Official

Georgia Coffman

OFFICIAL BY GEORGIA COFFMAN

First Edition © 2022 by Georgia Coffman

Second Edition © 2023 by Georgia Coffman

All rights reserved.

This is a work of fiction. Names, characters, organizations, places, events, and incidents are either products of the author's imagination or are used fictitiously. Any resemblance to actual events, locales, or persons living or dead are entirely coincidental. Any trademarks, service marks, product names, or named features are assumed to be the property of their respective owners and are used only for reference. There is no implied endorsement if any of these terms are used. Except for review purposes, the reproduction of this book in whole or part, electronically or mechanically, constitutes a copyright violation.

Editing by Amanda Cuff, Word of Advice Editing

Cover Design by Kate Farlow, Y'all. That Graphic

Chapter 1
SAMANTHA

A strained noise escapes my dry mouth as I sink into the movement, welcoming the burn running through my legs.

My muscles scream.

My heart thunders in my head.

I rise again, but this is shakier than the last, as expected.

Roughly exhaling, I blow loose hair out of my face, but it's no use—it sticks to the sweat on my forehead like a fly in honey.

It's so damn hot.

"That's it, baby," Jason says from behind me, his arms out in front of him with palms up to catch me if I fall. "One more. One more for me."

I blink the salty droplets out of my eyes and go down once more—ass to grass, as I always coach my followers.

Lungs squeezing and legs wobbling with each step, I barely make it to the rack. The barbell is so heavy across my shoulders that I'm sure it's leaving an imprint. Jason follows closely behind and helps me set the bar back in place until I limbo my way out from beneath it.

"Shit," I hiss, tilting my head back and placing my hands

behind my neck, where my fingers get tangled in my matted hair.

I don't know why I bother throwing my hair up, anyway. The wild strands always find their way out of the bun on top of my head. By this point of a workout, it's too heavy with sweat to stay there.

This is partly why I record my videos at the beginning of my workouts. It's when I have the best hair, form, and ability to talk in full sentences while I give followers tips and ideas to change up their routines. By the end of my sessions, I can barely stand, let alone speak coherently.

Contrary to popular belief—rather, what I callously lead people to believe—I work out hard, and it's not pretty. I encourage them to be their true and authentic selves, but at the end of the day, I know they don't want to see my pink bra turn dark purple from boob sweat.

The fact is, people want the shiny parts of my life on social media, and outside the gym itself, I have a lot of those parts.

I have a small condo in Santa Monica that I can afford because of my Instagram family, which has recently reached two million people.

I travel a lot too, everywhere in the United States and beyond, posing in front of the bluest waters or the most breathtaking mountain views.

And I even have enough savings right now at twenty-six years old to stop working for a while.

But my day-to-day is not glamorous. It's messy behind the scenes, and I have the tears of my body accumulating on my upper lip like a bathtub to prove it—just not to the public.

Instagram is for beauty, after all.

"You did it, gorgeous." Blood stops rushing so quickly to my ears, and Jason's voice eases through the thick fog over them.

Slowly, the sounds of the gym come back into focus too.

Clinking metal, heavy breathing, and loud counting of reps from workout partners.

"That was brutal." I give Jason a weak smile, my heart still racing, and not just from his naked abs on display thanks to him chucking his shirt during his set.

While his abs are, in fact, chiseled and glorious, I'm more riled up from this session. It was an adrenaline rush. With Jason's help, I pushed myself to surpass a couple of personal records, and I mentally pat myself on the back.

No matter how sore I'll be tomorrow—and I'll definitely be can-barely-walk-to-the-mailbox sore—it was a morning well spent.

I wrap my arm around his bare waist and lean in to kiss his lips, but he shies away at the last second.

"Whoa, whoa. Before we can do any of that, you need to take care of this." He draws a circle around my face, and I immediately frown. "I'm just saying—that workout was intense, and it's showing."

"Right," I mutter and withdraw my arm from him. Rubbing my fingers together, I note his sweat on the pads of them, but instead of calling him out on it, I ignore the urge and sling my bag over my shoulder as I head to the locker room.

He's just messing around, anyway. It's what he does.

Jason doesn't like to mix bodily fluids unless we're in bed, and it makes sense. It's logical and fair, even.

But why does it still bother me?

I finish washing my hands and return to the main part of Gold's Gym, the Mecca here in Venice. This place has it all, including every machine imaginable. Beyond that, I swear the energy swirling in here from fitness legends past makes me work harder.

Briefly closing my eyes, I thank my body for another good workout. After all, I'm young, but I'm not immune to muscle tears and joint pain. Another workout means another day to make my body and mind stronger—I'll take as many as I can get.

I glance to my left and right, but Jason is nowhere to be found.

Checking my phone, I see a message from him that says he's waiting outside in the car. I roll my eyes and adjust the strap of the bag on my shoulder with one hand and dab at my forehead with my towel in the other.

As I emerge into the large parking lot, the sun beams down on my flushed face as if to warn me it's the beginning of summer. Like I didn't already know.

Drained, I make my way to his truck, my legs stiff. Couldn't he have at least driven to the front door to pick me up? I'm not incapable of walking, although my leg workout might beg to differ, and I'm not the high-maintenance kind to demand constant chivalry, but *damn.*

What is going on with him?

I slow my pace as a sinking feeling settles at the bottom of my stomach.

He doesn't want to be seen with me.

I'm the one who suggested we keep our relationship a secret. Since we started dating, I've referred to him as "Gym Bae" online, and it's taken off, much to my surprise.

All I wanted was a little privacy. Before Jason, my dating life was more unreliable than my dad's Pontiac Trans Am. The pile of metal is older than I am.

I didn't anticipate how popular the whole secret boyfriend thing would get. I especially didn't plan on creating a whole brand around the idea, but people seem more intrigued by this mystery than they are the three prisoners who escaped from Alcatraz in the sixties.

I've started offering merchandise with a #GymBae logo, and it sells like crazy. At first, I handled all the orders myself, but I eventually had to contact a third party to ship them since my condo was beginning to look like a warehouse.

After a mishap with the first company and a shipment of inappropriate misprints—rookie mistake on my part—I found the right one to take my business to the next level.

This thing with Jason has been an ongoing trend to have fun with my followers, and their wild guesses always make me smile. It's hard not to when they comment with anyone from married celebrities like Chris Pratt to local bodybuilders.

But last week, I started receiving messages and comments from long-time followers that they're growing impatient. Some even insinuated it was all a lie to drive more traffic to my page and website.

Although it's not a ruse, it's been hard to argue with them. Honestly, I agree that the mystery has run its course, and when I told Jason as much last week, I expected him to be thrilled that we didn't have to continue being vague and coy online. I believed becoming publicly exclusive would help his following grow too, but even that didn't sway him.

He insisted we keep our relationship between us. His own half a million followers don't know he's dating anyone at all, and when I tried to talk to him about it, he kissed my neck the way I like and distracted me.

When I reach Jason's truck, I barely have the strength left to hobble into the seat. "You couldn't pick me up? My legs are toast."

After he finishes typing on his phone, he winks at me and finally says, "You skipped cardio today, so it did you some good, right?"

I raise my eyebrows and throw my head against the back of my seat as we drive out of Venice Beach toward Santa Monica, the palm trees along the way tall and comforting.

Once we stop in the parking lot close to my condo, more

sweat has accumulated on my back, and I'm in desperate need of a bath. A smoothie for energy. And I'm overdue for a massage, which sounds fantastic right about now.

Hoisting my bag up, I jump out of the truck, but Jason doesn't follow. He's on his phone again, and when he does look up, he wiggles his eyebrows. "Want to shower together?"

My eyes widen. "Seriously?"

"Yeah. Why?" He shrugs, then turns the truck off, and without the added rumble of the engine, my heart pounds even louder in my ears.

"I have work to do. Maybe I'll see you later." Scoffing, I slam the door shut.

I march up to my front door, passing the vibrant colors of my flower bed on the way. They usually put me in a good mood, which is why I planted them in the first place, but they're not doing much for me now.

And my mood worsens when I hear Jason's truck rev up again right before he drives away. Did I actually think he'd follow me inside and apologize for being an asshole today?

He's always joked around and made sexy requests, which I used to find charming, but something's off.

Sighing, I enter my home through the front door and lock it behind me. My first stop is the kitchen for a protein shake, which I drink on my way to the bathroom. Inside the white-tiled shoebox, I grimace over my sticky skin and turn the hot water on. As the room fills with steam in a sauna-like fashion, I peel my sweat-drenched clothes off, wincing with every lift of my finger.

My workout was killer, and I can't freaking wait to post about it.

I mentally sift through the different versions and captions I can use as I scrub my skin clean, the smell of eucalyptus mint soap soothing my body as much as it does my senses.

Afterward, I wrap my robe around me on the way to the couch, where I tuck my feet under me, turn on music through my Bluetooth speaker, and pull up the video from today.

But five seconds in, I realize I can't use this and groan. "What in the actual hell?" I mumble to the empty space as I fast-forward through the entire video.

Yep. The whole thing is useless.

I'm wearing my new purple leggings, and they are definitely *not* squat proof.

Shit, shit, shit.

Apparel companies constantly send me stuff to try on and promote for them on my platform. I'm grateful they trust me to advertise their products, but I always try them on first in the comfort of my own home in order to avoid what's happening in this video.

My ass is on display every time I even take a step, let alone squat, because these leggings are super thin and transparent. My damn leopard thong is as visible as it would be had I walked in there without pants on at all.

Maybe it's not *that* bad, but it's... bad.

I knew better. I fucking knew better than this.

I would've given them a test run before I left this morning had Jason not come over in a rush, claiming we had to get to the gym because he already took his pre-workout and needed to hurry.

Muttering to myself, I open my Instagram app and check my drafts for any fitting content to post today. Yesterday's post was a selfie, and the day before that was a quick reel of me in my new #GymBae merchandise.

A leg workout would've been perfect to share right now.

I go back and click the video from today—the one with my leopard thong on display—to see if any of it is salvageable. I scroll to the second clip and focus what energy I have left on manifesting a post-worthy version of it. I'd accept a frame I can at least screenshot at this point, but it's no use.

A knock on the front door jolts me upright, and I practically jump out of my skin.

As I stand, I drop my phone on the floor and scramble to pick it up when there's a second knock. My brother's voice rings out, "Sam, open up. It's me."

I set my phone on the coffee table with a thud, rush toward the door, and swing it open. Teddy leans on the doorframe, his hair sticking out to one side like he ran his hand through it repeatedly right before he arrived on my doorstep.

"What're you doing here?"

"Hello to you too." He smirks, brushing past me and into my condo. "Got anything to eat? And I mean real food. None of that organic vegetable shit you try to claim is *as yummy as it is nutritious.*"

"First of all, I haven't used the word *yummy* since I was five, and second of all, my *shit* is nutritious." I close the door and follow him past the entryway table toward the kitchen. "Third of all, why don't we just go out to eat? I can get a salad."

"Or burgers. When was the last time you had one of those?"

"Two weeks ago for my cheat meal." I stick my tongue out at him and toss my hair over my shoulder. "Besides, you eat enough burgers for the both of us."

"Ouch." He spreads his arms wide, then searches through my cabinets and makes gagging noises.

I like to tease him, but the truth is, he's more ripped than many of the guys who train at Gold's Gym. Even Jason would kill for my brother's biceps.

"Fuck." Teddy slams the last cabinet shut. "Okay, let's go out to eat, but Jason is not invited."

I cross my arms in front of me and tilt my head to the side. "Why not?"

"Sam, seriously, that dude sucks. I figured you would've dumped his ass already."

"He's not after my followers. I thought we proved as much since he hasn't mentioned online that he and I even know each other, let alone that we're dating."

"That doesn't mean shit. People are fucking crazy when it comes to followers these days. Did you know a hotshot influencer was mobbed at a grocery store last week? His *followers* broke his rib and chipped a tooth."

I study him. "That didn't happen."

"It did! You think I just made that up? I'm a storyteller now? That's Xander's job."

"Even if you're right, all that incident proves is that Jason is trying to protect me by keeping us a secret. You should respect that." I give him a smug smile.

I *so* got him there.

"Fine. Forget the influencer—that's probably fake, anyway. But believe this: Jason is bad news." Teddy leans on the counter, and the tattoos on his upper arms peek out from under his short sleeves. It's just enough to make out the tip of a flower petal, and if he'd raise the fabric any higher, I'd see the rest of a lily.

"You just don't like me dating anyone." I roll my eyes.

"Well, sure, but I really don't like that asshole. It's even in his fucking name, sis. Jason Douche." He grimaces like he just ate one of my healthy meals.

"It's Douché, like touché, and you know it." I drop my arms to my sides. "I'm going to get dressed."

"Okay, but I'm changing the music. Your tunes make me want to cry."

Walking backward, I try to fight my smile and my sarcasm, but fail miserably. "Have I told you how happy I am that you're here?"

"Don't need to. It's written all over your face."

On the way to my room, I pick my phone up from the coffee table and gasp when I look at it... and the hundred notifications littering my screen.

"What? You don't like James Taylor? Because if you tell me you don't, we have to have a serious talk."

I barely register what he says, along with the change of music. It's all muffled as I open my Instagram app and scroll the comments on my latest post—the one I didn't realize I even shared.

The video of me in my purple fucking see-through leggings and my leopard fucking thong on display.

"Sam?" Teddy approaches me and waves a hand in front of my face. "Hello?"

"Oh my God." I watch the end of the unedited video, where Jason comes into the frame, and I cover my mouth. "Oh my freaking God."

Underneath the posts are various comments, ranging from sleazy to pearl-clutching judgmental.

Sweet cheeks, lady.

Bring that ass (and thong) over here later.

Gross. This is borderline porn. Unfollowing.

"Okay, now you're scaring me." Teddy wiggles the phone out of my white-knuckled grip, and his eyes widen. "What is this?"

"That would be my very own Janet Jackson scandal." I run my hands through my damp hair as I slowly break out of my shock-induced trance.

"You can see your entire ass!" Teddy throws the phone onto the couch like it's poisonous, then covers his face with both hands. "My eyes!"

"Seriously?" I screech and run to the phone. Scooping it up, I fumble with it and open my Instagram again. "Delete it. I need to delete it. Where is the damn delete option?" I ramble under my breath until I find the button, but it takes more attempts than necessary to push it since my trembling fingers keep clicking on the wrong thing. "There. The post is gone. It's fine." I toss my phone back onto the couch and shrug.

I turn to Teddy and find him still rubbing his eyes.

"You can open your eyes now, *child*." I wrap my arms around my midsection, subtly tightening the robe around me.

"I know." He groans, and he continues blinking like the time he got sand in his eyes during our friendly game of beach volleyball last week. "But I accidentally stabbed myself with my finger when I went to cover them the first time."

"Like I said—you're a child." I snicker and go to my room to change, my nerves still rattled.

I take deep breaths like I do when I practice yoga, inhaling and exhaling to the rhythm of my movements as I change into loose jean shorts and a cropped tee. I don't know where Teddy and I are going to eat, but I'm positive it won't be fancy.

After all, it's Teddy and me. We're casual ninety-nine percent of our lives.

And this is Santa Monica. Beach attire is practically a requirement around these parts.

After I apply a single coat of mascara to my lashes, I toss my wavy hair into a bun on my head and exit my room. Teddy's antsy energy immediately hits me, and I stare at him as I cross the cold tiled floor toward my sneakers.

"What is it?" I ask over my shoulder.

"Um..." Teddy paces by the couch, one hand scratching the back of his neck while the other scrolls through his phone. "Do you want the good news or the bad news first?" he asks, lifting his hesitant gaze to meet mine.

I ignore my shoes and put both hands on my hips, fully facing him.

"Good news it is. Well, you look *ravishing*." He squeezes his eyes closed, then smiles, but it's the sarcastic one he gives when he asks for big favors. Like last summer when he begged if he and his friend Xander could crash on my couch.

What was supposed to be a two-day arrangement turned into two weeks of them taking up my space with their piles of dirty laundry and filthy dishes.

"What's going on?" I inch toward my big brother, my eyebrows raised. "You're blinking way too quickly, and you're one second away from sweating as hard as Nick Miller on *New Girl* when he lies."

"Fucking hell." He finally turns his screen around toward me, and I snatch the phone from him.

My face and—*gulp*—my ass are plastered all over it.

Memes and GIFs galore.

All from my fuck-up video.

"What the hell?" I gape at Teddy like this is all his fault.

"I'm just the messenger, okay? And the receiver. Quite a few of my friends have sent me those." He shrinks away from me like I'm one second from exploding.

Which isn't too far off base.

"You told them to delete it, right? Please tell me you did." I grip his phone, ready to throw it at the wall.

"They did. But what about the rest of the world?"

I spin in circles and tug nervously at the bun on my head. "How did this happen? It was only up for a few minutes!"

"This is what happens when you share your life with millions."

"Don't start with me."

"I'm not—"

"You are!" I hang my head. "This is so embarrassing."

"It's the internet, Sam. Let's face it—they'll have something else to laugh about by tomorrow. You'll see. Why don't we go drink? It's only four, but that just means we have a lot longer to get wasted before last call."

"I'll need several drinks and a new identity under witness protection."

"I can't do the last one, but I'll gladly take care of the first."

"Asshole."

"What did I do?" He wraps an arm around my shoulders and leads me toward the door.

As he swings it open, letting in the dull light of the early evening sky, my phone vibrates with a new text from my best friend.

Val: What the HELL is going on?

Val: I saw the video. Are you okay?

Val: I'm out of town with poetry Simon, but the minute I'm back, we're going out for drinks.

Val: Call me.

I quickly type to thank her—or at least I think I do.

I'm in a daze.

One so strong that not even the remaining sunshine hitting my face can pull me out of it.

I'm the laughingstock of the internet, and I'm sure it'll only get worse by the time the sun sets.

But that's a problem for tomorrow's Samantha. Right now, my only job is to forget the whole mess.

Chapter 2
XANDER

"What do you mean?" I blink at my boss, Ronald.

"You're fired, Alexander."

Fuck, he full named me.

"There's literally only one thing that could mean." Flustered, he waves his hands around like a cartoon lunatic, and his face is blotchier than when he's drunk—and he's a sloppy drunk. "You need to go. Grab your shit and get out. I never want to see you again."

He's one huff away from blowing the whole studio down, and I bet if I called him Ronald McDonald to his face like we do behind his back, it would do the trick.

But I refrain.

What good would it do? Then again, what would it hurt? I'm already fired, right?

I open my mouth, but Zoey steps in front of me. "Daddy, you can't fire him. We're in love!"

Cringing, I back away, ready to make my escape from this tension, but Zoey grabs my hand and loops her arm through mine.

"Please let him keep his job," she so stoically insists, but little does she know, her efforts are in vain.

Ronald wants me here less than I want to be here myself.

When I first started working here as a writing assistant, I thought it was a good idea, but considering how attached this girl has gotten to me, I'd say this firing has come at the most opportune time.

"Honey, he's manipulated you into sex, not love. Trust me, I know his type." Ronald throws me a glare.

"You don't know him like I do!" she whines.

"I know enough—"

"I'll let you two hash it out." I give them a tight-lipped smile and rush off before either one has a chance to stop me. Didn't feel like they were talking to me, anyway.

It's their problem now.

As for me, I grab a donut from the snack table on my way across the set, with cameras and a million lights aimed at me like I'm on a Broadway stage. People mill about, sipping their coffee, reading through scripts, and minding their own business as the director and his daughter continue their heated discussion in the back.

Zoey was fun, but love? *Jesus.*

I've never even been to her house, and the only reason I know her last name is because it's plastered all over LA for a new show premiering this winter.

So, no, we're most definitely not in love. But fucking? Yes. That's a much more accurate description of what we were doing, and we were damn good at it.

I tainted every inch of her dressing room like I marked her skin with my tongue and bites. She liked living wildly with the creative help, and we gave a whole new meaning to mixing business with pleasure.

It was working out swimmingly too, until Zoey convinced herself she's in love with me and told her "daddy," aka director, aka big deal, about me.

And now, I'm out of a job for the summer. How am I supposed to spend my days? With my fucking stepdad and his golfing buddies while they make boring jokes about shit that happened twenty years ago?

For God's sake, they don't even know what TikTok is.

No.

No fucking way am I putting up with that torture for the next three months until I take a seat at the table in my own writing room.

My damn dream job of writing for a TV action drama—it's finally happening.

Obviously, it was time to get out from under Ronald's clutches, but I imagined it would happen differently. For one, I expected to quit on my own terms. Maybe even storm out, leaving a swirling trail of script pages in my wake.

But this works too.

Once I'm in my truck, I pull my phone out and dial my best friend, Teddy. The second he answers, I say, "Dude, shit hit the fan with Zoey, and I've been fired. I need to get hammered, stat."

He tells me to meet him and his sister at Tito's, a lowkey bar in Santa Monica.

I check the time. "I'll be there before you take your third shot."

"Better hurry. Sam is prepared to set a drinking record, so it could get wild."

"Even better, man. Even better."

Forty-five minutes of traffic and seaside driving later, I throw my truck into park in front of Tito's and rush inside, but not before I get a good, strong whiff of the salt in the air.

I already feel free.

Teddy and Sam turn toward me at the same time as if they choreographed it like two people might in a horror film—my specialty. Before I sit, I wave to the bartender and order a double shot of Patrón on the rocks.

"Zoey burned you, huh?" Teddy asks, fist-bumping me in greeting.

I nod to Sam over his head and take my seat on the barstool. "She *torched* me. If Ronald rats me out and smears my reputation across this city like a disease, I'm screwed."

Teddy snorts into his drink. "Yeah, right. Even if Ronald McDonald posted your crazy sexual appetite on a billboard, you wouldn't lose your writing position. Your mother would intervene. I don't know the woman well, but I do know you don't mess with Delia Reynolds."

I smirk and thank the bartender when she sets a tall, dark, and strong drink in front of me. "You're right."

"She'd beat Ronald over the head with her five Golden Globes."

We laugh, but when I catch Sam's frown as she looks at her phone, I halt. "What's with her?" I whisper.

"Have you not been on the internet today?" He eyes me doubtfully in the same way Sam often does when I use too many analogies.

She hates when I do that.

"No. I was with Zoey at lunch, and then you know the rest." Once I pull out my phone and click on Safari, I search Sam's name, ready to see a bunch of her fitness posts per usual, but what comes up makes my jaw drop.

On display are her ass cheeks as she squats, and her leopard thong practically waves to the viewers. When she's done, she turns toward the camera and smiles. It's innocent.

It's obvious she has no idea people will be reposting this as they laugh at her expense.

They're calling her Sweet Cheeks Sam.

"Damn. This is brutal." I click my phone off, suddenly acutely aware that the ass I'm staring at in the videos belongs to my best friend's sister. But that doesn't stop the videos from playing in my head. So I take a big drink in hopes that it'll help. "What happened?" I manage.

Sam sets her empty drink down with a thud, annoyance emanating from her like steam out of the espresso machine at my apartment. "I just didn't get enough attention and needed to put my ass out there for more. That's how I get famous. It was the plan all along." Her sarcastic tone is dejected, and she slumps in her chair.

"She and Jason broke up," Teddy chimes in.

"Fucking asshole." Sam throws back a shot, then waves for another.

Her brother turns to me. "Mr. Douche doesn't want to be tainted with her humiliation, so he bounced."

"Not the whole story." Sam swivels around on her stool to face us. "He's embarrassed to have simply been in the video. At the very end. For two seconds." She scoffs and angrily swipes at the loose hair on her cheek.

Teddy shrugs. "I tried to tell her he's bad news."

"Seriously?" Sam slams her palms on the bar, drawing the attention of a few patrons, but she doesn't take her eyes off her brother. "This isn't like the time you told me not to eat the food truck taco during our trip to Mexico. This is my life. You don't get to say *I told you so* like a jerk."

"Don't take this out on me." He waves his hands in surrender.

I lift my short glass to my lips for a drink, staying out of the sibling duel of bickering as I revel in my relief. The burning tequila slides down my throat with ease, and it tastes even better now that I'm free. Considering the hold her dad has on her, I don't suspect I'll be hearing from Zoey anymore, much to my benefit.

I'm fine with confrontation when I break up with women—not that our relationship is so serious as to warrant a full discussion. Usually, a text will do, as that's the mutually agreed-upon extent of how serious we ever are.

It's the aftermath—the long succession of pleading messages I receive a week or two later—that makes me uncomfortable.

It helps that I've usually already moved on to someone new by then.

I lick my lips and speak up. "Do we need to wrestle for the title?"

"Title?" Sam quirks her eyebrow at me and purses her lips. I've hung out with her plenty of times to know it's her I'm-binge-drinking-because-I'm-pissed-off look.

It doesn't happen often. She claims the empty calories aren't always worth it, but every now and then, the unfairness of the world wreaks havoc on her positivity. When that happens, she turns to tequila.

But tonight is much, much worse than a shipment of dicks printed on her merchandise or walking in on two people doing it in her bed after a wild party.

So, I make this quick.

"The title of who buys the rest of the drinks for the night," I explain with a sly lift of my lips.

Teddy cuts his eyes at me and tosses back, "Or, we can just dig into *your* deep pockets to pay for the drinks."

"And shots," Sam adds, curling her long fingers around her new drink. "I need something stronger. My phone is still going off, and I barely have a damn buzz."

"Turn your phone off." Teddy snatches her phone and digs

into her miniature backpack—one so small it'd be more useful to an elementary school girl—but freezes. "Oh, fuck."

Her eyes widen. "What?"

"Mom called and wants you to take Reggie to the vet tomorrow."

"Not a chance am I going anywhere near that mangy lizard."

I hold a finger up. "Lizards don't actually get mange since it's usually caused by parasitic mites in mammals. It's rare—"

"Dude." My friend shakes his head at me and puts a hand up on one side of his face to shield himself from Sam's wrath.

Her glare is pinned on me as strong and fierce as a bad tattoo. "As I was saying, I'm not going anywhere near that *disgusting* lizard. Is that better?" she asks, directing her rhetorical question toward me.

Their parents brought home the lizard from the pet store last month like they were bringing home a newborn baby. It was wrapped in a blanket and everything. Teddy showed me pictures, or else I wouldn't have believed it.

The lizard was the newest addition to the reptile wing of their house, joining Rattle the frog and Rico the snake—their parents are cooky like that.

"Why can't they take Reggie?" Sam asks.

"I don't know. I only have the information in this text, which is what I just told you."

Sam grabs the phone from him and stuffs it into her backpack as Teddy's phone goes off.

"Oh, yes," he draws out, tapping on the screen. "I need to go."

Sam and I both whip our heads toward him.

"What happened to drinking all night, man?" I furrow my brows.

"Nature calls, and by nature, I mean my dick."

"What?" Sam's sip spills down her chin, and she uses the back of her hand to wipe it off, her pale pink nails bright against her tan skin.

"Bianca's home alone for the first time all day and wants to get it on." He wiggles his brows, gulps down the rest of his drink, and stands.

I laugh. "You know her son is only a couple years younger than you, right? You likely went to the same high school at the same time."

He shrugs. "She's a cougar and knows her way around a bedroom, okay? Much better than the fresh meat you go after. Why don't you join me in the big leagues?"

"You both know I'm still here, right?" Sam waves sarcastically and twists her lips.

Normally, she's bubbly and quick to make teasing jabs at Teddy's—and my—expense.

But tonight is different.

Instead of roasting on her brother and betting us she can fit more peanuts into her mouth than Teddy and me put together, she's sulking and drowning in tequila.

Gone is her usual spark and playfulness.

And damn, I hate to see her pout.

"Yeah, yeah." He smirks and kisses her on the cheek. "Love you, Sam, and Xander, buy my sister however many drinks she wants, and make sure she gets home safe, okay?"

"Got it." I nod and slide onto the newly empty stool, the outside of my thigh touching hers.

She blows out a breath, and her cheeks deflate as her posture shrinks. "You don't have to stay. I know I'm not much fun right now, so I won't be offended if you leave."

"On the contrary. Drinking happens to be my favorite pastime, and I have nowhere to be. You heard I got fired, right?"

"Aren't we a pair of winners?" She laughs, but there's no humor in it.

It's nothing like her laugh on any other day.

And I'm determined to be a good friend and stay at this bar until I make her forget the shitty day she's had.

Chapter 3
SAMANTHA

I scrunch my nose, wincing as sunlight filters through my blinds. The only reason I keep them open is because I want to see the sunshine first thing in the morning. It's part of my "rise and shine" lifestyle initiative, where I encourage followers to wake up with a positive attitude and win the day. It's something I practice myself, and it's helped me get to where I am.

A big part of fitness is mind over body, anyway.

But right now, I want to grab the sun and use the moon to squash it to death.

"So bright," I mutter into my pillow.

Slowly, I turn onto my side more carefully than if I was lying in a canoe and afraid of tipping over. My head hurts worse than any other hangover I've ever experienced, complete with throbbing against my temples and chills down my body.

Oh, and drool.

I wipe at the corner of my mouth and lick my dry lips. I must've slept with my mouth wide open, but that didn't stop tequila-infused drool from slipping down my chin.

"Fantastic," I say under my breath in a scratchy voice.

Instead of getting up to do my ten minutes of meditation, I pull the covers up to my nose and close my eyes, fully prepared to give in to sleep.

Especially when yesterday comes crashing back into my mind like a freight train.

The humiliation.

Asshole Jason, which he will be known as from here on out.

He freaked when he saw his face in the video and only called to tell me we're over. He didn't ask how I'm doing or bother to sound sympathetic at all. Just flipped out as if I did it on purpose because "I was so desperate for people to know I'm dating Jason Douché," as he put it.

Like I care about his name or brand. News flash: I have my own successful business.

I've been building the Samantha Ray online brand for over four years, and it's been lucrative since way before Gym Bae or Jason became part of it.

It *was* profitable, anyway, but my livelihood and reputation took a major hit yesterday.

If I get up, I'll have to address the video and lack of responsibility on my part to test the leggings beforehand.

My followers trust me to make legitimate and affordable recommendations on the best supplements, vitamins for women, and healthy recipes, but above all, they want to see what gym attire I love.

When I first started out and went from Samantha West to Samantha Ray, I only had fifty followers, made merchandise myself with a secondhand press machine, and posted poorly edited videos. I knew as little about cultivating a strong brand as I did running ads.

All I knew was that fitness changed my life. It gave me the confidence to be my best self and strengthen my mind, body, and soul. I wanted to do the same for others, so I learned from all my failed attempts at marketing and ruined T-shirts.

I kept climbing and built my empire through my profile, merchandise, supplement sponsorships, and more.

Entrepreneurship 101: have multiple avenues of income.

And I did have several avenues, all of which have now been tainted with a single innocent mistake.

Xander did a kickass job of distracting me last night—and giving me a killer headache—but he's gone.

And I have to face reality.

Groaning, I scoot farther into the blankets, ready to crawl out of my skin at just the thought of the heap of damage control ahead of me.

I don't even know what step to take first.

"Oh, you're up," a man's voice sounds from the door of my bedroom.

I shriek, shooting upright, and my back hits the headboard.

"Relax." Xander enters my room, his dark hair sticking out in every direction like a mad scientist with a softer edge.

And more ab muscles.

He's also dressed in the same clothes from last night, where we drank ourselves into oblivion.

Or at least, I thought he did. He's smiling too widely to be hungover.

"Did you sleep here?" I croak, my throat so dry it hurts.

"I thought about going home, but then I saw the fluffy blanket out there on your couch and thought, *Gee, I bet that's comfortable.* And it was. It really was." He hands me a mug, steam rising from the hot coffee inside, which makes me smile.

It's like a reflex—I see coffee, and it automatically makes me happier than the shining sun through my blinds.

"There. All better." Xander sits on the edge of my bed and

places his hand on the other side of my legs on top of the comforter. "Drink up, and let's go."

I lick the bold liquid from my bottom lip and frown. "Where? If we made plans last night, I don't remember, but I definitely have to cancel. I'm not leaving this bed."

"Oh, but you don't want to miss a trip to Maui."

I lift an eyebrow, cupping the mug in my lap between both hands. "Did I black out? Because I'm positive we never talked about Maui."

"You told me you want to get away for a while and hide out on a beach in peace with plenty of food and drinks. What's a better place to do that than Maui? It's perfect." He claps, and his grin grows wider.

I blink.

He doesn't budge.

After a beat, I hold the mug of coffee high over my head and kick my legs out from under the comforter, throwing them over the edge on the opposite side of him until my feet sink into the carpet. Once I'm standing, I whirl around on him. "Are you insane? I can't go to Maui. I have to... to..."

"To what?" Xander rises from the bed until he reaches his full height over a foot above me and crosses his arms in front of his broad and lean chest. "Sam, you said it yourself last night that you need a break. You haven't been on vacation since you and the fuckwad Jason *Douche* went to Vail over the winter, and you can't look back on your last trip and think of him."

"I said all that?"

He crosses the short distance between us and squeezes my shoulders. "You need a breather, and I need to occupy my summer anywhere but here. I can't be stuck in my stepdad's house for three months. I'll suffocate. Do you want that on your conscience?"

I roll my eyes. "What happened to your house?"

"I'm subletting it to a friend who just moved to LA. Teddy's searching for the perfect place for him to buy, but until then, I told him he could stay at mine. I thought I was going to be working long hours this summer during filming and could crash at my stepdad's. In small doses, he and his ideas of jokes are fine, but I can't take long hours with Klein. The man has a last name for a first, for fuck's sake." He rubs a hand down his face and peers over at me. "None of my plans are working out, though. Not after yesterday."

I nod, suddenly remembering he was fired. It's all coming back to me in pieces.

"You and I have known each other for a few years now. I stayed here for two weeks last summer, so you know we can stand to be around each other for long periods of time. It's exactly the escape we both need." He shrugs like he's got it all figured out, and it's hard not to get excited.

How can I not get caught up in this fantasy he's describing?

On top of that, it's not like I have a boyfriend to keep me here.

And I could use a place to clear my head.

He grabs my free hand in both of his strong ones as he peers into my eyes in a way that feels too intimate for two friends, but it's hard to dwell on it when he says, "When we look back on this moment in fifty years, trapped in a soul-sucking retirement home, don't we want to be able to say we did something crazy fucking fun instead of bailing on a trip of a lifetime like a couple of suckers?"

I worry my bottom lip, chewing on his proposition like he asked me to move in with him. But it's only a short vacation, right? To freaking Maui.

Sweet paradise.

Why am I not saying yes?

"Say yes," Xander pleads, a sparkle in his eye and a pause in his breathing.

"Okay, let's do it." Smiling, I spread my arms and realize too late that I'm still holding a full cup of coffee. It spills over the edge, the warm drops splattering across the tops of my feet and the carpet.

"Fuck it. You'll clean up when we get back." Xander nudges me toward my closet.

"I need to clean that before it sets." I set the cup on top of a coaster on my nightstand. "Besides, what's the rush?"

"I already bought us two tickets, and our flight leaves in two and a half hours."

"We're not going to make it. Traffic alone will be ridiculous. And I need to pack, cook and eat breakfast, do my yoga and meditation—"

"Grab a swimsuit and your passport. We'll stop for coffee and bagels on the way. You'll meditate on the plane. Maui, Sam. *Maui.*" He whispers the last word, and his lips twitch with similar excitement to the energy fluttering in my chest.

His enthusiasm is infectious.

"Maui," I repeat, smiling wider than a whale during feeding time.

In the name of vacation, I pack like the wind, even faster than I thought I could move. Without time to plan, I pack way too much, so I toss out a few pieces of clothing I know I won't need. I just want my favorites, anyway.

I still have to sit on top of the suitcase to zip it.

"And done," Xander announces like he has a stopwatch in his hand.

He yanks on the bag, and I slide off with a yelp. "If I would've known vacation mode makes you this crazy, I might've reconsidered."

"Too late!" he calls over his shoulder, my suitcase rolling behind him with a gurgling sound.

One of the wheels needs to be tightened, but he refuses to stop. I chase after him, fumbling to find the right key to lock up. Then we race through the courtyard to the parking lot, where we both come to an abrupt stop.

"Oh, fuck." He places his hands on his head and spins in place, letting out a groan that echoes around us. "My truck is at Tito's, which means we have to take your damn Prius."

"Seriously? You want to miss our flight to Maui because my Prius isn't good enough for you?"

He studies the compact car, doubt coloring his features, and after what feels like an unnecessary amount of time for such a tiny decision, he holds his hands out. "Give me the keys."

I toss them to him and rush toward my eco-friendly car with my head held high. Once inside, he taps on his phone in his lap, then checks behind us and peels out like they do in the movies, stray rocks flying backward with the force of two determined people.

A muffled greeting sounds from Xander's phone from an unfamiliar voice.

"Klein, can you please get my truck from a bar? The spare key is in my room on the dresser, and I'll text you the address." He slides his hands along the steering wheel as he takes a turn onto a busy street.

"Sure thing, bud," his stepdad chirps. "Where are you off to?"

"Maui." Xander flits his mischievous gaze at me.

"And who is the lucky lady you're sweeping away to such a romantic place?"

"It's not like that." He rubs his chin, and the previous glimmer that was there disappears. "I'm going with Sam. You know, Teddy's sister."

"Of course, of course. You two have fun, and I'll take care of the truck as soon as Jerry finishes grabbing his mail across the street. If I leave now, he'll certainly stop me, and we'll be stuck discussing the pickleball match yesterday." He groans. "I'm not a sore loser, but losing to *Jerry* really stung."

"Tough break." Xander shakes his head, and his cheeks turn red from stifling a laugh, which he lets loose as soon as they end the call.

"Wait!" I grip his thigh, and my hand barely covers his hard quad. "What about your stuff? You don't have any clothes or even a toothbrush."

A sly grin spreads across his face. "I have my credit cards, and they're all I need. I'll buy new stuff. I mean, I just need swimming trunks, flip-flops, and sunscreen, because all I plan to do is drink on the beach and swim. Maybe snorkel."

"What if we go hiking? Because I definitely want to go hiking."

He shrugs, more nonchalant and collected than a sloth. "Okay, I'll buy sneakers."

"You're very calm for someone who's just lost his job *and* girlfriend."

He gasps. "She was not my girlfriend. How dare you," he says, his voice laced with sarcasm.

I burst into laughter. "Zoey St. Claire is crazy famous, though! It wouldn't be the worst thing to be associated with her, especially in your position."

"As a new writer for serious TV? Yeah, being tied to a girl who's barely legal to drink and is on track to be the next *Hannah Montana* isn't exactly what I've aspired to all my life."

"I'll give you that." I lean back in my seat as we merge onto the interstate toward LAX. "Why did you take a job as an assistant, though? You don't need the money, since you're legit rich. I mean, we're jetting off to Maui on a moment's notice, for God's sake."

"You have my Venmo information, by the way, so feel free to pay me back for your half. We have the next several hours, so you have plenty of chances." He chuckles, and the glimmer in his eyes matches the sparkle across the ocean in the mornings.

It reminds me of the way he chuckled last night, so open and free.

The sharp dip of his upper lip came and went as we laughed over silly things—there were a lot of those. He seemed to be on a mission to make me forget the day I had, and he did a damn great job of it as we traded stories of our pasts.

I never realized it before, but Xander's a good listener.

I shift in my seat as I peek over at him. "Technically, you invited me, so…"

He bursts into laughter, and although I have every intention of paying him back the moment we get to the airport, I enjoy teasing him.

After all, he can afford twenty tickets to Maui without blinking. His mom's done well, making a name for herself in Hollywood for years. His stepdad is a hotshot tech developer, who's too smart and intuitive to be human.

That's how Xander describes him, anyway.

Being an only child, Xander has reaped the benefits of his parents' good fortune and has been well on his way to making his own. This new gig will just keep the ball rolling for him.

"Are you going to answer my question, or what?" I lift my eyebrow.

"I needed to prove myself and network with the right people. Flashing my birth certificate hasn't always been enough, so I went the more practical and hardworking route. You know, paid my dues and shit. But I messed up with Zoey and am afraid

I lost a lot of points with some of my colleagues." He rubs his jaw, and remorse rolls down him in waves.

"Everyone makes mistakes," I offer lightly, honestly surprised that he feels guilty over something like this.

Xander Logan isn't exactly the type to dwell over heartbreak.

I've never actually witnessed him ache over any woman he's gone out with in the three years I've known him.

"You'd think I'd know better by now," he mumbles and squints in the mirror as he switches lanes. "Plus, I just..."

I angle my body toward him and hold the seat belt out from digging into my shoulder. "Yeah?"

He leans an elbow on the window and rubs his chin, his square jaw clenched—wait, is he nervous to tell me? Seriously? He's never shy around me.

This has to be some parallel universe because the Xander sitting next to me is not my brother's best friend that I've come to know.

"Okay, you're being weird," I tell him. "And now you *have* to tell me."

"I like being on a set," he blurts, but I don't get it.

"You're a screenwriter. Of course you like being on a set."

He shakes his head, fumbling over his words worse than I imagine a first-time actor might. If I'm being honest, it's kind of endearing. "It's more than that. I feel like... Sets are... It's like this: you feel at home in the gym, right? It's your safe place. Your happy place. It's where you feel the most like yourself. You get a rush, even."

"Yeah," I whisper, my teasing grin faltering.

"It's how I feel when I'm on a set. In the writers' room. Anywhere near a production, no matter if it's the next *iCarly* or whatever."

I gulp—I know the exact feeling he's describing, and it's a

powerful one. There's something about the thrill those happy places can provide. The inspiration the air sparks. The comforting feeling of being in the right place at the right time.

It's special, to say the least.

"I didn't intend to get all sentimental." He laughs softly and runs his hand through his tousled hair. "It's stupid."

"It's not." I squeeze his jean-clad thigh. "It's not stupid at all. I can relate."

He nods, but he doesn't take his eyes off the road. If I could get a good look at him, I'd likely see the full extent of his sentiment.

I've witnessed Xander's vulnerability in the past, but it's been in fleeting glimpses. Nothing like this moment where he draws me in and makes me part of an obviously personal and intimate experience—one we can both share in, at that.

A fuzzy current of warmth meanders through my chest as we settle into easy conversation again, in between him cursing other drivers, anyway. At one point, he lays on his horn, muttering under his breath, "Fucking turtle-driving road hogs."

I cover my mouth, laughing. "What does that even mean?"

"Oh, they know," he says, weaving through cars like a Formula One driver.

I'm relieved when we make it to the airport and through security in time for boarding. One of my sneakers is still untied by the time my ass hits my seat on the plane, but it was worth the risk of tripping over it.

Because we made it.

"You can tie your shoe now," Xander says, pointing to the thick laces.

"I thought you were going to leave me if I took the time to do it out there, especially after we already wasted time after the wheel on my suitcase popped off," I throw back.

His light-hearted grumbles are barely audible as a flight

attendant comes by to confirm we have our seat belts on and trays in the upright position.

When I sit back up from fixing my sneaker, I catch her cheeky gaze landing on Xander as she compliments the tattoo on his wrist.

"I've always wanted a tattoo on my shoulder, or elsewhere." She narrows her gaze suggestively, and her innuendo is more obvious than the hair on my head. "I'll be back to check on you after takeoff."

When we're alone again, I whisper to Xander, "I bet she looks back at you at least three more times before she takes her seat."

"Doubtful."

"I wouldn't—oh, there's one." I notice the flight attendant's coy glance at him before I finish my sentence. "And another."

He shifts next to me, and his knuckles brush the outside of my bare thigh as my shorts ride up my leg. We're cramped in this space, and I can't afford to make it tighter by inflating Xander's ego with this little game.

But I just can't help myself.

It's taking my mind off yesterday's debacle better than any glass of rosé or tequila shot.

He and I both look up at the same time and find she's gazing back at him again.

"I win." I shrug as the overhead speaker dings on.

"You never told me the prize, so there's no bet. No winner, either."

"The prize is a trip to Maui." I tilt my head toward him. "I thought that was obvious." I throw my head against the back of the seat and laugh, careful not to rattle the passenger to my right.

I'm already glad I agreed to this ridiculous and spontaneous adventure.

Once we're in the air, I lean over to ask Xander, "Oh, by the way, how long are we going for?"

"That is up to us. I only booked us a one-way flight." He gives me a sly grin.

"I like the sound of that." I squirm in my seat, my hangover long gone. It's replaced by giddy excitement, instead.

I spent most of yesterday moping over my public wardrobe malfunction as Samantha Ray.

Today, I'm Samantha West.

Just a girl on a plane to Maui with her brother's best friend.

Chapter 4
XANDER

"You're in Maui with my sister? What the fuck, dude?" Teddy's voice echoes through my phone's speaker.

"I believe the locals say *on* Maui," I say, a touch of sarcasm in my response because I just love to push his buttons. That's what friends are for, right?

His loud sigh is heavy, and it sounds more like static crackling from an old TV. "When were you two planning on telling me?"

"Now?" I lean my hip against the bathroom counter.

It's been two days since Sam and I landed on the island. Two days of sunny paradise. We've spent so much time on the beach that I'll probably never be able to wash the sand and salt out of the crevices of my body.

And it's pure fucking *bliss*.

I'm here with a good friend. Aside from the online shitstorm she's ignoring, she's drama-free, unlike Zoey and some of the other women I've gone out with over the last year.

Sam is also funny and easy to talk to.

We're the perfect traveling pair, which bodes well for me, especially. I needed this break from reality as much as she did.

"Are you sleeping with her? I swear to the universe and beyond, if you say you are, I will tell every woman in Hollywood that your dick is smaller than a cornichon. Better yet, I will cut your dick off and feed it to you. I will—"

"Shit, man." Chuckling, I wipe the mirror with the heel of my palm to clear the fog from my hot shower. "No need to do me any harm. We're just here to blow off steam and nothing else. You know I don't think of her that way."

"You're still a guy, though. And we always think with one body part. It's why you were fired, remember? It's also why I'm in a clusterfuck myself and stuck between two cougars. They're playing tug-of-war with me, and I can't lie—it's a damn turn-on."

"What's the clusterfuck, then?"

"They found out about each other and are making me choose."

"I thought you were just messing around and that they agreed it's for fun. Are they saying they want more?"

"I guess they think with one body part too. Except they'd rather eat carbs than share me."

"Didn't think you had anything against carbs."

"I don't. Hell, the more, the better. But these rich house-wives make it a competition to see who can lose more weight postdivorce."

"I can see why you're so attracted to them," I deadpan.

"You should worry more about yourself than me," he clips. "I will bury you in Davy Jones's Locker myself if you lay a finger on my sister. Christ," he mutters. "I just watched *Pirates of the Caribbean* with Bianca's kid niece. I'm really losing it here."

"I promise I won't send you over the edge—Sam is off-limits, and you have nothing to worry about with us. Chill." I pick up my phone to end the call, but add, "Oh, and I'll remember your vivid imagination when I need help with revenge plots on the show."

"I'm your man. As long as you keep your fucking word."

"Always do."

The call goes silent once he's clicked off, but Teddy's warning continues echoing in my head.

I run a hand through my hair, slinging water droplets onto my bare shoulders. It reminds me of earlier when Sam flung her long hair backward as she came out of the water.

She turned several heads and caught the attention of countless men, married ones included.

I couldn't blame them, either. There's a reason she's so successful doing what she does—she captures people's attention easier than a crab snaps its claws.

I meant what I said to Teddy about her, but I'm not blind.

Although she and I always have a chill and fun time together, I don't think of Sam in any sexy scenarios. Not because she's not hot as fuck, but she's always been my best friend's sister. My own friend, even.

In other words, an impossibility.

When it comes to women, I steer clear of complications, and crossing the line with Sam would be beyond messy.

I glance at my phone again to check the time and confirm I have one hour until dinner by the beach.

We made reservations at the hotel restaurant that boasts of seafood as delicious as the suites are luxurious. Not their exact words per se. I put my own spin on it since I know that statement to be true, firsthand.

I'd tried the lobster there when my mom, stepdad, and I visited Maui years ago, my first and only other time here.

After Sam and I secured our rental, I drove straight to the same resort and crossed my fingers that they had two adjoining rooms available. The other stipulation was that they had to have a patio with a view of the beach, and even though June is a busy month for the island, we were able to snag a couple of premium rooms.

Sam claims I sweet-talked the young woman at the front desk, and she couldn't resist my flirtatious responses to her questions, but I denied it the entire walk to the rooms.

Besides, who cares how we got them? For this view, I'd gladly charm a large, hairy dude, or even let a damn shark in my personal space.

Holding a fluffy towel around me, I enter the main part of my room, and the yellow and white leis we got on the day we arrived immediately catch my attention. They're bright and match much of the vibrance of the room.

Beyond the bed, a sliding glass door leads to the patio, and the bushes surrounding it are trimmed and neat. The color of the flowers among the greenery matches the leis too.

I secure the towel above my hip bone as I walk toward the sliding door, the outside and the beach both calling to me. I spend a lot of time at beaches in LA, but they're nothing like the ones here. The swaying palm trees, chaotic cliffs, and clear waters. The air of quiet paradise. I can almost always hear tunes of the ipu and ukulele everywhere I go.

It's so relaxing. I haven't thought about the ordeal with Zoey even once.

I pull the sliding door closed behind me and step up to the gate, leaning my elbows on it and getting lost in the music of the island.

It looks and sounds the same as I remember, although it's more lively now. Perhaps that's because the memories have faded, since my last trip here was almost ten years ago, but still. My parents had brought me here as a high school graduation present, and although we had our fun, there were plenty of downfalls too.

My mother and Klein worked as if we were still in LA, but

the plus side was that I had a lot of free time to write. Nothing more inspiring than a beach view and a virgin-cocktail alongside easygoing tourists soaking up the sun.

It was definitely better than the time I was fifteen and tried to write at Venice Beach. A strange woman dressed in dirty clothes with sand smeared across her cheek marched right up to me, ripped a page out of my notebook, and blew her nose in it.

The worst part was that she balled the piece of paper up and threw it at me like I was a trash can.

In any case, this trip will be very different than the last.

While I may or may not have already made a few notes in my character book about the woman at the front desk, I'm determined to make this vacation more about the fun.

"Xander, I was just coming—"

"Sweet... Cheeks Sam!" I practically jump out of my skin, whirling toward Sam's voice as my heart thunders in my ears.

"Are you seriously making 'Sweet Cheeks Sam' a thing?" She grimaces, but her expression quickly transforms as she drops her gaze lower. "Oh, um, you..."

She brings both of her hands to cover her eyes and spins in place, right, then left, and back to the right as if too much sun has blinded her.

What the hell? I peer down and realize my towel fell off, and on display, is my junk.

"Shit," I hiss and bend at the knees to scoop my towel back up. Once my cover is secured, I face her again and find she's blinking more rapidly than a malfunctioning taillight, her cheeks flushed. "You can look now. I'm decent."

She clears her throat and rubs her neck, her gaze still darting everywhere but directly at me.

"What's going on here?" I wave over her.

"Nothing. It's nothing... I mean, I've seen it before, so it's not a big deal."

"You've seen my dick before?" I place my hands on my hips. "This is news to me."

"Once." She shrugs. "It was last year when you and some girl decided to go skinny dipping. In my hot tub. I was definitely home, by the way."

I scratch the back of my head, racking my brain, and finally, I recall the night Delilah and I had a couple drinks and decided to Uber over to Sam's, where we jumped her fence. "Fuck. Teddy had mentioned you got a new hot tub, so..."

She crosses her arms over her chest, which is when I realize how low cut her pink dress is. Her cleavage is mouthwatering.

If she was any other woman, that is, but again, I'm only a human guy. I can appreciate a nice pair of tits, no matter who they belong to, right?

"And you thought it would be fun to break into my place to use it," she finishes sarcastically. "Were your parents' bajillion-dollar pool and hot tub and the entire ocean in your backyard not good enough?"

I squeeze the towel around me, rocking on my heels as embarrassment colors my cheeks. "You should be flattered that we found your place to be far more exciting."

"Right." She rolls her eyes. "I didn't get in that thing for over a month. Had to bleach and disinfect it about a thousand times since I knew you had sex in it."

"I'm offended." I clutch my bare chest in exaggeration. "What makes you think we did anything scandalous?"

She scoffs. "You were naked with a woman. And you're *you*, so there's no way you kept your hands to yourself."

"Damn. You caught me." I give her a sheepish grin, suddenly ashamed.

Sam knows I'm no saint and that my past is filled with not-so-stellar indiscretions, but knowing she saw us that night makes me feel... icky.

I've never felt this way about any of my actions until now. *What the fuck?*

"Let's never talk about it again, okay?" she offers, and her tone is genuine.

I sigh in relief. "Deal."

"Now, what I was coming over to say is that I'm ready if you want to go ahead to the restaurant. There are hammocks hung between trees on the way, and I want to get a few pictures for my page. But, clearly you need another minute." She points at me.

I run my fingers through my hair, which is now dry, thanks to the evening breeze. "I'll be two minutes, tops."

She taps her watch. "I'll be counting."

***

"**R**ight here." Sam points to a spot between two tall trees, and the pink-and-yellow hues of the sunset filter through the green leaves and long branches, casting a gentle glow around us. "What's cuter—lying in the hammock or just sitting in the middle of it?"

I open my mouth to answer, but she claps her hands.

"Wait! I got it." She hands me her phone, which is covered in a case that matches her pink nails, and the combination makes me smile.

It's very Sam to match her shit like that.

I turn the camera toward her as she heads for a hammock, taking her shoes off along the way. I follow her, but she stops me when I'm a few yards away. "Stay there and snap a few shots."

"Why, I'd love to. Since you're so polite and all." I hold the phone up and peer over the top at her.

She curtsies, pulling her flowy dress out to the sides, her

bright pink toenails peeking through the blades of grass. "Please, Mr. Logan, can you take my picture? *Please?*"

"That's more like it." I laugh, and the camera shakes, making her and the background blend into a mosaic of different colors.

She points to my right, diagonal from where she sits in the middle of the hammock, and asks, "Can you please, sir, take the picture from there, please?"

"Are you going to do that all night?"

"You asked for it." She sticks her tongue out and sways in the netted material like it's a swing. With each push-off, the higher her dress slides up, revealing more and more of the line of defined muscle of her upper leg.

Before she glances down, I catch a glimpse of her glowing eyes, and her naturally wavy hair blows in the breeze over one lean shoulder, letting free strands flow over the other side.

And I snap the shot before she tells me she's ready.

I check my handiwork and nod. "You're a natural."

"I didn't do anything." She looks over at me, her eyebrows furrowed.

"That's why I said natural." I tilt my head with an underlying *duh*.

She licks her lips and reaches up to tousle her hair, loosening the curls at the end. "A couple more after I'm ready." She eyes me and adds, "Please, Sir Xander."

I chuckle and wait for her signal as a few people pass behind me, murmuring about a snuba excursion they went on this morning. I'm immediately interested in hearing more, but Sam draws my undivided attention back to her.

And she hasn't even said anything.

She scoots farther back onto the hammock until her feet dangle in front of her, her bare heels and toes barely grazing the ground. A soft wind sweeps under her dress again and lifts the material just slightly, like it's keeping the color of her panties a secret.

I find myself leaning in to find out.

"Did you take it?"

Are they pink like her toes?

Is she wearing a thong like in her viral video?

"Hello? Earth to Mr. Logan," she calls out to me, sitting upright.

"Hmm?" I clear my throat and shift from one foot to the other. "I'm ready. Tell me when."

She gets back into position and looks away from the camera, her glossed lips barely parted, her skin tan and radiant.

I never really knew the meaning of the word *sun-kissed* until now. Until I stare at Sam and her golden-brown skin, her legs long, lean, and toned.

Like a gift from the sun itself.

It's hard to take my eyes off her, but once she gives me the go-ahead, I manage to snap a few shots.

She smiles, and I take a few more, feeling like I'm intruding for some odd reason, even though she's the one who asked for pictures.

At the end, she hops up, grabs her strappy sandals, and sashays toward me, an extra bounce in her step that I hadn't witnessed before we got here.

It's like taking a few pictures by the beach is better than lying on it. Does she really enjoy this more than the water tickling her toes while she sips on sweet specialty drinks out of coconuts?

When she reaches me, I ask, "You like doing this, don't you?"

"It's fun. It makes me feel like I did when I modeled a few years ago." She grips my shoulder and uses it to balance herself as she slips her sandals back on.

I quirk my brow. "Modeling, huh?"

"A couple years before Teddy met you and brought you into our lives—"

"Much to your excitement." I wink.

"—I was picked up by an agency." She smiles, a twinkle in her eye like the sparkling stars making their appearance now that the sun has started to set. "They hooked me up with a few gigs, and although I had a good time, it wasn't for me. I felt so much pressure to stick to a strict veggie diet and cardio routine. But I fell in love with weights somewhere in the middle, and I didn't fit their mold anymore."

"Your agency dropped you?"

"I decided to pursue other avenues," she says sarcastically, like she's quoting a manual. Which I infer to mean they didn't *officially* let her go, but they did prompt her to quit. "It worked out in my favor, anyway, because I can lift weights and still model. But this is better since I can do it on my own terms and call the shots myself. I don't have to deal with an agent's nasally commands to eat my celery."

I chuckle as we walk side by side toward the restaurant, brushing shoulders with other vacationers every so often.

I fall into step beside Sam and realize I'm still holding her phone. Handing it back to her, I ask, "Do you want to check the pictures to make sure they're okay?"

"I trust you." She tucks it away inside her tiny purse and shifts it around so that the dainty strap is draped across her chest, nestling deeper in the valley of her breasts with each step.

Once we reach the restaurant, the hostess shows us to our table, and along the way, we pass tall windows, through which the water of the sea is barely visible. Flickers of moonlight dance across the top, then disappear with each wave. The linen-clad tables are decorated with votive candles that cast a pinkish glow.

It's such a simple accent to pull the ambience all together, and the view does the rest.

After we're seated in a corner booth with a view of the ocean in front of us, I lean in and say, "You're very good in front of the camera. Have you ever thought about acting? You'd be perfect for this screenplay idea I have. A suspenseful thriller of a young woman who accidentally kills her father, but when she tries to hide her trail, she discovers her father's really—"

"Ah! *Spoiler*." Sam glares at me, her mouth open.

"Like you're ever going to watch it."

"Then why would you ask me to be in it?" she challenges.

"Being in it and watching it are two different things."

"Okay, but why would you think I wouldn't watch it? I like... some... of those kinds of movies." She shifts in her seat, amusement brightening her features as she toys with the ends of the silverware in front of her.

I smirk. "You hate anything that doesn't make you laugh or swoon."

"*Swoon?* Seriously?"

"Tell me you don't swoon over *The Notebook* every time you watch it, and I'll buy the most expensive bottle of wine this place has to offer—hell, I'll buy a barrel of it."

She chews the inside of her reddening cheek. I'd think she's blushing, but we've gotten a lot of sun the last couple days. It could easily be a sunburn, or a trick of the pink glow from the candle.

But I'd bet she's blushing because it's obvious I'm right.

"Exactly. You swoon over romantic bullshit. Take it from me —screenwriters know all the right ways to make women fall in love with movies. They play into those emotions and tug at them like puppeteers. It's comical, really."

"There's nothing wrong with liking romantic comedies or romance, in general, for that matter. It's nice to watch a hopeful movie, where no one dies in a horrifyingly gruesome murder." She stares pointedly at me.

"How do you know the woman kills her father in a violent murder? I didn't say that."

"I've read some of your stuff. You're twisted."

"It's art." I fight a smile. "I want to be the next Stephen King, but instead of writing long-ass books first, I'm going straight to the screen."

"I thought your TV show would be more like *Law and Order* and other detective dramas." She peers questioningly at me.

"That show is, but it's not the only thing I want to do with my life." I drag my tongue across my bottom lip, then sigh. "I've been shopping a few screenplays around town to see who bites, but Hollywood moves slower than a turtle crossing the street. It took two years to land the TV job, no matter how many favors and connections my mother called on."

Thankfully, my debacle with Zoey hasn't been as damning as I feared. Since Ronald fired me, the only text I've received was from one of the other writers, and it was just a GIF of Leonardo DiCaprio laughing hysterically.

All in good fun—that's basically Brian's life motto.

"Aloha." Our server comes by with a pitcher of water and fills our empty glasses. He then places two wineglasses in front of us and retrieves a bottle of white from the tray. "Would you like to try our specialty wine made right here on Maui? It's a fruity sparkling pineapple wine that will impress your taste buds more than Makani will impress you two with his fire dance."

I exchange an intrigued glance with Sam, and we both nod at the same time.

"My pleasure." Once our glasses are full, he whisks off toward the bar.

"How are you doing with the breakup?" I squeeze Sam's arm across the table.

She offers me a small smile, but it's sad—nothing like the one she gave me on the way here.

We haven't mentioned the drama she left behind. As far as I know, she hasn't taken her phone off airplane mode, and I haven't checked her platforms for any comments on my own phone, either. Every time I've started to, I stop because I don't want to intrude or cross any lines.

When she's ready, she'll handle it herself, but I bring it up now just so she knows she can talk to me. That I am her friend, and I care. There's an urge in my chest to make sure she knows.

"You can't seriously tell me you wanted to be Samantha *Douche*, did you? Come on." I attempt to give her a soothing, crooked grin, but it might appear as more of a cringe. Because, who would want a fucking name like that? "If you ask me, it's the best thing to happen to you."

"It's Douché, and no. I didn't want to marry the guy, but did he have to be such a jerk? I thought we really liked each other. We had a lot in common. Similar goals and senses of humor. We made sense."

"Barf. Barf. And double barf."

She tilts her head back and laughs, and it's far better than the sad smile she gave me moments ago.

It feels damn good to get Sam in better spirits.

"I know you're a romantic optimist, but I'm going to let you in on another little secret." I lean forward, and her sweet scent invades my senses, catching me by surprise.

"Please do," she whispers, her half-smile animated.

"Love and relationships are for boring dumbasses. Not for people like us." I point between us, my voice gravely sober. I swipe the stem of my wineglass and take a sip—I need it if I'm going to keep getting so sentimental with her.

"Right. We just go out with exciting dumbasses for fun."

"Anything's better than boring." I wink over the thin rim of my glass.

When the server comes back, we place our entrée orders, and I'm surprised—confused, really—that Sam orders a salad. Did she not hear what I said about being boring?

She at least has the decency to add fresh shrimp on top, so I'll let it slide... for now.

As soon as we're alone again, I slide my glass aside and lean forward. "Any changes with the video?"

Even though we haven't talked about the video since our plane landed, the damn replay of it slammed into me like a thousand bricks when she sat in the hammock.

The image of her thong in my head just... appeared. But that doesn't count as far as promises to her brother are concerned, so I'm in the clear.

In any case, the buzz of awareness along my hot skin that the thought alone incited is for me to know, and me alone.

"I haven't checked my phone other than to make sure my pictures are clear and that my ass cheeks are not showing." She giggles, but there's a nervous air about it.

I slide my hand away, desperately trying to keep images of said ass cheeks out of my head. "Have you thought about what you might say once you're ready? Do you have a publicist or something?"

An exhale leaves her with a whoosh like the waves crashing on the beach, but this is much less calming. "No. But it would make this a lot easier if I did."

"Why don't you?"

"Social media is my job. I'm the influencer, and I want people to know me as a person, not what some faceless marketing guru thinks is best for me to act like. I want to be real, and shit happens to real people. I just have to face my mistake."

She sips her wine, and after a brief pause, she says, "Eventually."

"Cheers to eventually." I clink my own glass to hers.

The soft music filters between us, and in my periphery, I see a woman dressed in black approach the table beside ours, then make her way to Sam and me. "How is the lovely couple this evening? Celebrating anything special?"

"Oh, no, we're not..." Sam starts, but her laugh interrupts the rest of the sentence.

"We're not together," I finish for her.

"Just friends. That's all." Sam holds her hands up as if to prove there's no funny business happening underneath the table or something.

The woman, whom I assume is the manager around here, clutches her chest with both hands. "Of course, of course. My apologies. Please let me know if you need anything at all. I'll be back in a few to check in."

Once we thank her, I glance around at the elegant restaurant and the dim view of the beach. The water glistens underneath the moonlight like this is a Nicholas Sparks novel, and Sam and I are sitting close to each other in the curved booth. During our conversation, we gravitated toward each other.

We're having a romantic candlelit dinner.

Two friends.

My best friend's little sister, to top it all off.

"That was funny," Sam says and sips more of her sweet wine.

I force a laugh and scoot toward the edge of the booth, putting distance between us.

Because I have a promise to keep, and it's not something I can half-ass, no matter how sweet and intriguing Sam's floral scent is.

Chapter 5
SAMANTHA

"I got the drinks." Xander holds up two coffees as best he can since there's a bottle of Kahlúa under his arm. "You have breakfast?"

I hold out the bulky tote with a giant pineapple on the front, which I bought from the hotel gift shop to serve as a picnic bag.

And this morning, I put actual pineapple slices inside it.

He sets the coffees on the counter of the kitchenette and gets to work pouring Kahlúa in each. When he turns back to face me, I take note of his T-shirt with a cartoon dolphin and a cloud above it that reads "Where have you *fin* all my life?"

Pointing at it, I snort. "What the hell is that?"

"Hotel gift shop clothes. Is it my fault each item is more ridiculous than the next?" He nods toward my quirky bag with a challenge in his smirk.

"Fair enough." I move to toss the two canvas totes over each shoulder, but he stops me.

"Take the coffees, and I'll carry the bags."

I swat at his hands. "I've got them."

"Come on. It's a lot. Let me be a gentleman."

I scoff. "You, a gentleman? *Please.*"

"Hey." He clutches his chest dramatically, as he does when he's joking, but there's a very real edge to his tone when he asks, "What's that supposed to mean?"

I tilt my head, and my smile falters. "No, it's just that, you know... you're as loose with the gentleman quality as you are with your pants zipper."

He lifts a brow, his lips curling at the ends. "Just because I enjoy a woman's company doesn't mean I don't take care of her. I pick her up for dates, open doors, pay for dinner, and cook breakfast."

"And in between all that, you tell her you're not looking for anything serious."

"No, that's the conversation we have before we ever go out. I believe in being upfront with my... desires. No need for false expectations." He shrugs. "Zoey just didn't listen."

I barely hear the last part.

Out of nowhere, I find myself licking my lips when the word *desires* falls from his mouth like honey. It's seductive, even though I don't imagine that's how he meant it.

Not toward me, anyway.

Xander has only ever seen me as Teddy's little sister. Hell, he probably thinks of me as his own sister. Why else would he have invited me to Maui for an indefinite amount of time?

He wouldn't have asked had he felt anything romantic for me. He doesn't usually go on a second date with a woman, let alone on a tropical vacation with her.

This is him being a good friend to distract me with delicious food, a few laughs, and plenty of sunlight and fresh air to replenish my soul.

It's working too. It's as if my stress has been carried off by the sea breeze like a Hawaiian magic carpet.

With Samantha Ray on the backburner and her drama trapped in airplane mode, I'm finding Samantha West again.

Here on the island, I can be myself again, and it's all thanks to Xander.

Suddenly, guilt turns my stomach.

"You're right," I say to Xander, my voice faint. "There's nothing wrong with a healthy sex life, as long as both parties are on the same page."

"Glad you see it my way." He winks and throws his hands back out. "Now, can I carry the bags, please?"

"No." I sidestep him toward the door, and he scoffs behind me. "I have my principles too, which include being capable of carrying my own bags. You're not intimidated by strong women, are you?" I challenge over my shoulder.

"I'm not." He holds his hands up. "I love strong women, but that's not the conversation we're having. I didn't offer because I don't think you're capable. I offered to be nice."

"I'm still carrying the bag," I insist, but it's more out of stubbornness than anything. After the stink I just made, it'd be weirder to accept his offer than it is to hoist the bags over my shoulders and carry them myself.

"Suit yourself," he says as he grabs the coffees and follows me into the hall.

As we walk, the taupe carpet and sparse paintings along the wall of the hall transform into sleek cream tiles of the lobby floor. The space itself conforms to minimalist décor, but it's vibrant too with the orange rug. A round table at its center serves as the focal point, and on top is a bouquet of unique and pointed flowers in a large, clear vase. When we checked in, the man at the front desk told us the flowers are called bird of paradise and that they're typical on the island, although not so average in appearance.

The middle of most of the flowers reach out like a bird's beak between orange-and-red petals as if it's emerging from fire, tall and proud. I've seen plenty of them in Southern California, but here, the bouquet seems bolder and stronger. I love walking through the lobby just to stare at them and draw strength from them myself.

I take one last breath of cool air as we step through the wide doors, the heat immediately covering us like a weighted blanket.

As we continue toward the beach, Xander leans over to try and peer inside one of the bags hanging on my arm. "What's for breakfast?"

I pat the tote. "Kale. Egg whites, which we should eat quickly before they get cold. Pineapple and orange slices too."

He blinks at me. "What else?"

"That's it."

He twists his lips like I just told him I have a fungal infection waiting for him inside.

"What? It's a healthy breakfast to get us energized and ready for the day."

"You ordered a salad last night when there was lobster and literally any other option. At lunch, you order pretty much the same thing too." He grimaces more deeply than if I'd shoved the salad in his face.

"I'm having seafood pasta later."

"Don't you preach about balance? This sounds like restriction, aka madness." He tilts his head and turns, leading us toward the beach.

"I *am* all for balance, and it's what I genuinely believe is best. But I've cheated a lot since we left my condo—remember the drive-thru on the way to the airport? I haven't had fast food in ages."

"And you loved it, right?"

"Of course. It was delicious and worth the stomachache I had afterward, but if I had biscuits and fried chicken every morning, it wouldn't be cheating or balance. I can't have carbs on carbs on carbs for every meal, or I wouldn't do what I do."

"You're on vacation, though." He holds one coffee out toward the ocean as if I'd forgotten. How could I?

I smile right about the time my toes hit the sand.

The sun is still rising, and the beach lies sleepily under the shadow cast overhead. A few people seem to have the same idea as us—a picnic with the scenic sunrise over the water. Most of the tourists haven't set up their chairs, tents, or speakers yet, and it's quiet and peaceful at the moment.

Aside from Xander's chatter, that is.

"Our vacation has no end date as of right now," I point out. "So, I can't cheat every day for two weeks, a month, or however long we decide to stay. That's the balance part. I'm having carbs today, but I'm holding off tomorrow. Which reminds me, feel free to join me on my runs."

He scoffs like I offended his mother. "I don't run on vacation."

When we find a spot to set up camp and he removes his shirt, my gaze falls to his abs, each one like it's carved out of stone. Turning around, he flashes me with the contours of his back, the ridges and grooves like the mountains on this island.

Men.

They can eat all the pizza in the world, exercise a few times a month, and are good to go. Especially guys in their late twenties like Xander.

Metabolism is a fickle bitch.

"We've been here almost a week and haven't discussed our plan, not that I'm in any hurry to leave this place." I uncover the egg whites and grab the plastic cutlery room service left me. "My parents are on me to come back for my dad's birthday in a couple weeks, but she said I can't have any cake. She calls it my punishment for taking off without driving Reggie to the vet. Little does she know, I'm happy not to eat cake. It's not my favorite dessert, and if I'm going to eat sweets, I'm going to make the calories count with ice cream or a cheesecake slice the size of my head."

He lets out a loud laugh that jolts me, the sound rumbling from deep in his chest. Over the last few days, I've come to revel in his laugh. It's carefree and makes me want to cover myself in it like a blanket.

"It's settled, then." He rubs his hands in front of him. "You'll give yourself a break."

"I am." Again, I wave around the ocean. "What you don't seem to grasp is that it's not about restrictions and making myself miserable. It's about showing people that living a life of balance is not only possible but also amazing. We can indulge every now and then, but sticking to healthy options for most of our meals is good for our bodies. We only have one, so we should take care of it."

When he doesn't immediately respond, I peer down at him where he lies on a towel on the other side of the food.

He's staring back at me, and his curious gaze makes me self-conscious. Is there something on my face?

"What?" I tuck loose strands of hair behind my ear.

"I like when you talk about your work."

"I'm sure it's like you when you talk about writing."

"I guess."

"Why do you write? I don't think I've ever asked you that." I take a small bite of my eggs, but I barely taste them. I'm more interested in his answer, strangely eager to know him better.

I'm actually surprised I don't know how he started writing. Before we arrived on the island, I thought I knew him pretty well, but I'm learning all these new things about him now.

And I like it.

"My dad got me into writing when I was thirteen." He tucks his hands behind his head and turns his attention toward the ocean, where the water is still and calm. The more he talks, the more the water lightens from the rising sun. "When my mom's acting career took off, she traveled a lot. Acting isn't a nine-to-five job, but my dad's finance job was. They were both gone frequently, which wasn't a big deal when I was in school. They just had no clue what to do with me during breaks, so my dad picked the first thing he could find on a list of *things to occupy your teenage son during summer*."

I raise my eyebrows, sensing a bitter layer under his tone, but I remain quiet.

"Little did he know, my dad's idea to get rid of me worked out in my favor. I almost hate that it's the one thing I have to thank him for. He didn't even stick around to see me through it." He laughs, but it lacks any trace of humor. "Anyway, when my first screenwriting summer program ended, I found myself still writing well into fall and winter just for fun. I wrote random scenes between classes and researched other programs to continue exploring that avenue, and now here we are." He spreads his arms wide, and a proud smile stretches across his square jaw.

I return his grin, at a loss for words.

This is one of the rare moments when I get this side of Xander. One where he's not cracking jokes and talking about his latest hookup.

When he's vulnerable and honest, he's captivating.

The first time I laid eyes on him, I never would've believed he's a writer had Teddy not told me beforehand. At first glance, the guy walks the walk of an LA actress's son, an aura of poise and certainty following him like the air he breathes. His thick hair is as dark as his eyes, but not as rich and deep. Those eyes hold more than stars for Hollywood.

The more time I've spent with him just the two of us, I've noticed the quiet way he studies the people around us through the eyes of a storyteller—with meaningful contemplation of what raw and flawed layer lies beneath the surface of perfection.

I study form in much the same way—following the fluidity of a movement like it's telling a story. One of internal gratitude and strength, albeit grueling too, the latter of which isn't too far off Xander's gritty taste in movie genres.

Maybe Teddy is the reason I know so little about his past. Usually, my brother's around to razz on him, which doesn't tend to leave room for a real conversation. Does Teddy even know some of this stuff about Xander?

Surprising me, Xander sighs and squeezes his eyes closed, reaching his hand out. "Okay. I'll eat whatever you give me. Be gentle."

Humming, I rummage through the bag and retrieve the other container of egg whites that room service brought me. Before I even hand it to him, I know he's going to hate them—after all, the yolk is the tastiest part of an egg—but I refuse to waste a perfectly good serving of lean protein.

He peeks at his palm and groans.

"Enjoy," I sing.

Grunting, he sits up and tears into his food like an animal. He usually eats more gently, but I suspect he wants to get it over with sooner rather than later.

"We have to start enjoying all that the island has to offer instead of just existing on this beach." He waves around us at the large expanse of white-sand mounds sprinkled with a handful of other vacationers under rainbow-colored umbrellas, hats on their heads and drinks or books in their hands. "We need to live a little."

"If this spontaneous trip itself doesn't count, then we definitely lived the other day when we had shrimp out of that food truck."

"That is a Maui institution, recommended to us by almost

everyone we encountered the first day we got here, including the flight attendant before we stepped off the plane."

"You mean the *flirt* attendant?"

He gives me a pointed stare.

"It was either that or Flirty McLoverson."

"Better than Sweet Cheeks Sam, I suppose."

"That's cold." I lower my sunglasses over my eyes and lean back on my elbows, my heels dancing into the sand near the edge of my towel. "You're the one who said all you planned to do is drink on the beach and swim, and you had the right idea. I'm having a great time doing just that."

"Maui has so many things to do, though. Snorkeling, hiking, and I heard from the concierge that there's a big wine and food festival next week."

"I'm here for the wine and food—sign me up." I make a motion with my finger in the shape of a check mark in the air.

"Oh! And there's this thing called snuba diving that I want to try." Xander sits up and rubs his hands together, his voice rising an octave as he asks, "Okay, what else? We need to make a list, and we can't leave until we do them all."

"Sea turtles. I've heard of this place where you can see a bunch of sea turtles. They call them *honu* here."

"Are you sure you're supposed to pronounce the *h*?"

"That's what our server called them the other night, and I trust him."

"I'm in." He retrieves a notebook and pen from one of the bags, and over his shoulder, I watch him flip to an empty page.

"What is that?"

"Focus," he murmurs, but I don't miss the layer of enthusiasm in his tone. Once he jots down the sea turtles and the festival, he adds "hiking" and "snuba" too.

After a moment, he taps the page with the end of his pen and says, "A pig roast. I want to go to a luau with a pig roast."

"Let's do it." My excitement rises with every item we add to the list, and the glimmer in Xander's eyes grows brighter too.

The truth is, no matter how awesome it is to lounge around the beach—in a gorgeous place like freaking Maui, no less—making this list has made me realize I've been moping on this beach instead of enjoying the wonders around me like I should.

But having something to look forward gives me the burst of optimism I need to start getting over this funk.

Even though I'm still in deep trouble. All it would take is a single swipe on my phone to see just how bad.

Just... not yet.

I'm having too much fun simply existing, as Xander puts it.

I know I need to face the humiliation, but every time I pick up my phone to do it, I turn it back off and run down to the hotel gym for a workout or lean my head back on a towel as the sound of waves washes over me.

I know it would help to talk to my best friend—she always knows the right thing to say. But I haven't even checked my texts or called Val since I left, so now I can add "bad friend" to the mix as well. She's going to absolutely kill me when I finally get home.

Until then, I'm going to enjoy the items on the list we just made like the end of the world is coming.

Xander might not be right about my vacation diet, but he's onto something when it comes to having a good time.

Because this has been one hell of a fun time, and it's mostly because of my company—my brother's best friend, of all people.

Why ruin it with the drama of real life?

Chapter 6
SAMANTHA

"Okay," Xander says, putting his phone in the bag. "I've called and reserved two spots for snuba diving, and when we get back to the hotel later, we'll ask about a pig roast."

"Sounds like a plan." I shift onto my back and stretch my arms over my head after a long morning of lying here. After we made our list, Xander got right to work making calls—it seemed like he couldn't even take another breath before he made our reservations.

"We also have to get our first real meal at some point today," he says over his shoulder as he shakes sand from his board shorts.

"What I brought was real," I argue, my eyes still closed behind my sunglasses. "I'm stuffed."

"Excuse me?" a feminine voice asks.

Xander and I look up to see a woman holding a volleyball.

"Would you like to play?" Her accent sounds European. I'd guess Italian, given her olive complexion and dark, silky hair.

We glance behind her to see a guy waving, and I smile.

"We'd love to!" I grab Xander's arm, and we stand at the

same time. "I'm Samantha, but you can call me Sam. This is Xander."

"Nice to meet you. I am Francesca, and he is Mario."

When we reach Mario by the water, we shake hands with him too.

Then I miss the first volley.

"I need to warm up," I announce in my defense as I wave my arms to the sides, loosening the muscles from a short but intense workout in the hotel gym yesterday. The lactic acid that's built up is making me stiff, and I didn't do myself any favors by lying still for the last hour and a half.

As the sun grows hotter and rises higher in the sky, we hit the ball back and forth over an imaginary net, grains of sand flying each time one of us lunges for the ball.

As more people claim their spots on the beach, the tide comes near us, and when we start splashing saltwater into our eyes, we find a new spot to continue playing.

"You have come here before?" Francesca asks in her heavy accent as Xander retrieves the ball I tossed into the water after another bad volley.

"I was little when I came. I barely remember any of it except for the clear water—swimming was my only priority back then." I giggle. "What about you two?"

"First time," Mario says, wrapping his arm around her. "Our honeymoon."

I clutch my chest over my bikini top. "That's so sweet."

When he reaches us, Xander's hair is dampened by the water. It drips down his face, falling from his black eyelashes in rapid succession and momentarily distracting me.

I don't have to admit out loud or fear Teddy's wrath to acknowledge to myself that the guy is very... hot.

"They're, um, on their honeymoon," I sputter. "Isn't that so romantic?"

Xander nods. "Oh, congratulations."

"Thank you, thank you. And you two?" Francesca raises her eyebrows.

"We're not together. Just friends." Xander gives them a tight-lipped smile.

Francesca brings her hands up to cup both of her cheeks. "But you are so cute together. Are they not, Mario? Look at them. So young and happy."

Xander squeezes the ball between his large hands, his body tensing. "Ready?" he practically bites out.

Our new friends don't seem to pick up on it, but it's obvious to me that he's bothered, probably by the fact that two different people have now mistaken us for a couple.

Eyeing him, I fall back into position, and we continue lobbing the ball back and forth for almost an hour as we chat about Italy and their house outside of Rome.

I almost ask what made them choose Maui. After all, it's a long trip to this side of the world, but when I glance around and think about it, who *wouldn't* want to come here for their honeymoon? I'd travel for a week to get here.

The vegetation covering the cliffs is greener than any kale or yard I've ever seen. The beaches are pristine and make me feel like I'm in another universe—a fairy tale, even. The energy is unparalleled too—warm, inviting, and exciting with *aloha* spirit floating in the air like fairy dust that brings smiles to everyone's faces.

It's amazing.

And the perfect place to escape to and forget the shitstorm that my life has become.

"Heads up!" Xander calls out, and before I can blink, the ball smacks my forehead, knocking me backward with a huff.

Francesca rushes toward me. "I am so sorry, *carissima*."

"I'm okay. No problem at all." I rub the spot above my eyebrows to ease the dull ache migrating through my head.

"Are you sure?" Xander pulls my arm to face him and inspects my head, his lips parted and eyes squinting like my forehead is as small as an acorn.

"I'm fine. Really, it barely smacked me."

"Smacked?" Francesca furrows her eyebrows and turns to Mario.

"Hit?" Mario explains, but it comes out as more of a question.

"Yes, yes. It did not hit me hard. I'm totally fine." I smile widely. "You're very sweet."

She tucks her curly hair behind both ears, and her uneasy smile holds a hint of concern, even though I'm attempting to reassure her it's no big deal.

Italians and their sympathy.

It fills me with warmth.

Smiling, I accept Xander's arms to help me onto my feet. We're about to get into position to continue playing, but Mario checks his watch and snaps his head up. "*Principessa*, our reservation for brunch."

"*Mio Dio*. I forgot." Francesca holds her hands up. "We must go."

"Of course. Have fun." I wave, and Xander walks the ball to them. "Thanks so much for inviting us to play."

"We will see you around, yes?" Francesca squeezes my hands, smiling expectantly. "*Belissima*."

I grip her hands back for confirmation, and when they leave, I turn to Xander. "How stinking cute and nice were they? I'm dying over their adorableness."

"I think that's the concussion talking." He lifts his eyebrow.

"You and your antilove ways." I roll my eyes.

I wouldn't expect anything else from the romance hater, so

I'm not surprised he wasn't swept off his feet with the young couple.

But he's not going to ruin my swooning.

That's right—I'm swooning, and I don't care who knows it. My love life might be worse than a rotting brown banana, but it doesn't mean I can't be happy for others.

And I'm happy for Francesca and Mario. They give me hope.

Since I'm loose and high on a rush of endorphins from chasing the volleyball around the beach, I head for the water instead of our laid-out towels. When my toes hit the edge of the cool tide, I call over my shoulder, "You coming?"

I make it hip deep into the water when Xander barrels in after me, wrapping his arms around my waist and tackling me into the water. Once I come up for air, I cough, fighting the sting of saltwater that seeped into my nose. "You ass!" I choke out, searching for him through my blurred vision.

He finally comes into focus again, and I lunge at him with every intention of shoving the smug grin off his face by using each ounce of force my weightlifting regimen has instilled in me.

Laughing, he falls backward with seemingly little effort.

I go to push him again, but he stops our water wrestling fun and stands frozen, staring at me like they do in horror movies.

Or *Jaws.*

"Oh my God, is there a shark coming toward us? Because I read that there have been some sightings of—"

He clears his throat and averts his gaze. "You, um... Your top is..."

I glance down and see my nipple.

My *bare* nipple.

My bikini top must've gotten disheveled when he pushed

me, and now my breast is hanging out right here in the middle of the ocean.

Does *wardrobe malfunction* need to go on my resume now, or what?

I dip into the water to adjust it and scoff. "Could you be any more of a teenage boy? It's a tit. You've seen one before."

"I know." He splashes me, and I jerk to the side, not that it keeps drops of water from hitting my cheeks.

"Besides, now we're even." I glance between his legs below the water, referring to the towel incident on our patio.

"Well, technically, you'd already seen my goods, so you owe me one more peek."

"Is that right?" I grin, shaking my head as my body hums with sudden awareness that I'm having this conversation with Xander.

Any time we've talked about body parts, my brother's been around, and they were talking about other women's "goods."

Not mine.

My brother's best friend wasn't alone in the ocean with me, either.

On Maui.

We have no buffer here, and it's easy to get caught up in the game.

"Yeah, so just show me the other tit, and we'll really be square." He winks, his shit-eating grin too wide and arrogant for his own good.

He's goading me with this dare—a challenge.

And I'm intrigued.

Before I can think better of it, I grip the other side of my top and fold it over, exposing my other nipple to him.

His jaw drops, and he stumbles back, losing his footing. Xander falls into the water, his mouth still agape as he goes under, and I'm certain he just swallowed a gallon of saltwater.

I laugh as he resurfaces, his shell-shocked expression still intact. Sticking my tongue out at him, I swim away.

Feels like a win when I can render a guy like Xander Logan speechless.

Even if it doesn't mean anything.

Which it totally doesn't.

Just an innocent dare.

"Did you forget how to swim?" I call from several yards away, where I come to a stop to slick back my wet hair. "It goes like this." I throw my arms out, one after the other, bobbing my head from side to side like the tide as I exaggerate each movement.

"Smartass," he says and meets me halfway.

I shrug and open my mouth for a snarky comeback, but there's a sudden splash that doesn't come from either of us.

The hair at the back of my neck rises.

My eyes widen in terror, and I feel the blood drain from my face as a shiver of fear travels down my spine.

Now this is what horror movies are made of.

Xander reaches for me right as another splash erupts from behind me, and a fin appears in my periphery. Shrieking, I propel myself the rest of the way into his arms and wrap my hands around his neck, clinging to him for dear life—literally.

"Oh my God, oh my God," I repeat over and over again, too petrified to turn around and be faced with—*gulp*—a shark.

"Hey, hey. Relax," Xander coos in my ear, his wet cheek pressed against mine. "Look. It's just a dolphin."

"What?" I blink, my heart thundering too loudly to comprehend his calm words.

"A dolphin," he says over another splash, but it's farther away this time.

I peek over my shoulder at the friendly mammal, who flips

its tail above the water a couple times like it's greeting us, then dips back in with a rainbow-like movement.

Graceful and magnificent.

"Oh." I let out a breath, and my smile slowly spreads.

A dolphin.

Relief seeps into every crevice of my body, replacing the fear running through my veins like an antidote.

I sag against Xander as we admire the creature in awe, remaining silent like we're too worried our voices will scare it.

Once it swims away and joins the other dolphins in the distance, who jump out of the water in sync, I exhale again, but this time it's with fascination. The kind of amazement I feel when I'm in the presence of something inspirational and peaceful.

It's too special for words.

"I've never been this close to a dolphin before. It was..." I stare out at where they continue swimming, popping out of the water for air and growing smaller with the distance.

"Beautiful," Xander whispers, sharing this experience with me.

I turn to face him, and immediately, our gazes lock. All of a sudden, my breath hitches for a totally different reason as I realize I'm wrapped around his body like a koala bear, my legs hugging his trim waist as my arms cling to his neck.

My stomach against his hard abs.

His strong arms holding me in place.

And his hands... Oh God, his hands.

I'm instantly aware that he's gripping both of my ass cheeks —my bare flesh.

My bottoms shifted when I jumped, acting more as a thong than a conservative swimsuit, and his hands are now spread across each cheek like they belong there.

But it's new.

Exhilarating.

When his gaze drops to my lips, a wave of excitement dances down my spine, and my senses heighten. Rushing adrenaline from what I thought was a near-death experience courses through me.

Is he going to kiss me?

My lips part of their own accord, inviting him in.

And I don't let go.

Chapter 7
XANDER

She pulled her tits out.

Her bare fucking tits.

They're bigger than I expected—have they always been that size? Big enough to fill my palms so I could feel the full weight of them?

I stare at her full lips and lick the water and salt off my own. What would hers taste like? Salt and lip gloss and summer?

Heaven?

I'm holding her like I'll drop her, when in truth, if we let go, we'd simply float apart. Which makes me hold her tighter, digging my fingers into her firm ass and enjoying the feel of her toned muscles, a glorious result from hours in the gym.

Eyes locked on Sam's, I lean in, my mouth only a whisper from hers, ready to find out exactly how she tastes...

But we're interrupted by a growling sound, rumbling against her tight body.

"What was that?" She breaks our staring contest and searches around us, goose bumps instantly sprinkling along her arms.

"That would be my stomach," I confess, disappointed that it fucking betrayed me.

The moment has passed, and I can't believe it's because of my damn stomach.

Then again, it's for the best. What was I thinking? Did I black out? I can't kiss my best friend's sister—no matter how badly it seemed like she wanted me to.

And I'd bet my hard dick that she wanted me to.

"Jumpy, much?" I ask, my voice husky.

Her round shoulders relax, and she loosens her grip on me, sliding her wet body away. "I was almost just killed by a shark."

"It was a harmless dolphin."

"I'm still not convinced you didn't find a real sea monster earlier and just aren't telling me."

"I saw something unexpected, that's for sure," I grumble.

I'm just not sure how dangerous it is...

Her lips twitch, and I've never been so eager to know what she's thinking. But she surprises me when she changes the subject entirely. "How are you still hungry?"

I search her expression, and the curiosity in her eyes and pinched brow leads me to believe she's not thinking about my stomach at all. "You fed me rabbit food. I'm in charge of meals from now on," I say, playing along.

If she wants to talk about food instead of what almost just happened, fucking fine by me.

After all, we're friends. Just *friends*.

"In that case, you'll be eating alone more often than not," she tosses back at me.

We continue bickering like this, settling into our usual dynamic—the safest place for us—until we reach our picnic. The beach is now filled with three times as many people as before, crowding the open area with multi-colored towels, gear, and coolers. Kids scream when their tiny feet touch the water, their squeals and giggles echoing down the shoreline like a megaphone.

The couple next to us whispers in each other's necks, occasionally macking on the other like they're in private.

And I'm jealous of them.

"Can you believe some people?" I mumble loudly enough for only Sam to hear. "There are children."

Sam follows my gaze toward the inappropriate couple now tonguing their way to the Bermuda Triangle. "Leave them alone. They're in love and happy."

I grunt as I shift on my towel, my ass forming a lopsided hole in the sand beneath me.

"You're just mad you're not getting any. Is this the longest you've gone without sex?"

I scoff. "No. I tore my meniscus in college and couldn't... *perform*... for weeks."

"*How* did you *survive?*" she asks sarcastically.

"With plenty of porn, masturbation, and more porn."

"Talk about inappropriate." Her voice is weak and low, drawing my attention to her and her pink cheeks.

Is she flushed?

I almost forget why we got out of the water—why I didn't fucking kiss her when I had the chance—until my stomach growls again like an alarm, reminding me to eat.

And that it was for the best that it interrupted whatever damn momentary lapse in judgment I had with the woman sitting next to me.

Thank God I didn't have real food earlier, because otherwise, I would've kissed Sam. She was practically begging for it. There was no mistaking her desire, not in the way she was holding on to me. I would've devoured her teasing lips without a care in the world for the consequences too.

Not only would Teddy have given me the ass-kicking of the

century had I made a move on his sister, but what about the rest of the trip? It would've just made things awkward, when everything's been going so well.

And I meant what I said about the list. I want to complete it as part of my determination to make this trip better than my last one here.

Besides, I don't know when I'll be able to return once we leave. Who knows what the future holds? The TV and film industry moves quickly, even if responses to pitches take longer than snail mail. I might get a call tomorrow from a producer who liked one of my scripts that they found as it meandered from desk to desk like a nomad.

So, the list is as important as a lifelong bucket list. But nowhere on it does it say "kiss best friend's sister in a heated moment of an adrenaline rush."

No, this is for the best.

Abso-fucking-lutely.

* * *

After several more rounds of groaning from my stomach, Sam and I pack our shit and walk to a café right off the beach. Lights are strung around the patio, which is enclosed by wooden beams that lie parallel above each other like a ladder. The faint echo of the waves mixed with loud wails of seagulls transforms into chatter and buzz from the other patrons as we approach our table.

Once we're seated in the corner, Sam pulls her phone out and swipes left like she's on a dating app.

The thought alone spikes my heart rate—and not in a good way.

"What're you doing?" I fight my urge to leap across the table.

Get a grip, man.

"I'm checking the pictures I took earlier and the ones from last night with the hammocks. This is the longest I've gone without posting to my socials, and I need to make sure I step up my game once I do get back to it." She bites her bottom lip, worrying it as she continues swiping, pinching the screen to zoom in every now and then.

My focus locks on her lips, noticing how plump they actually are, and immediately, I recall my up-close-and-personal view of them from before.

"Aloha. Welcome to Ohana Café. What can I get you to drink?"

I jerk upright. "Hey, hi, hello."

Sam eyes me from across the table, then smiles warmly at the server as she gives her drink order—water. Why am I not surprised? The woman is basically an endless well of water, drinking and basking in it with satisfaction. I'm still stunned she even drank the coffee with Kahlúa I gave her earlier.

I must say, though, it's endearing. I might give her shit because I like to mess with her, but Sam is a damn inspiration.

Even so, I like to bask in the opposite during vacation. "Bloody Mary for me please."

Once she scurries away, Sam dips her head. "I know what you want to say."

I freeze with my grip crippling the laminated one-page menu.

"You agree with Teddy. That I should've picked a different career, boyfriend, and condo. Hell, I'm sure you and Teddy would love to do my grocery shopping too. But I'm happy with my choices, okay? I don't need sweet alcoholic drinks every hour in order to enjoy a vacation."

"Whoa, Sam." Instinctively, I reach across the table and squeeze her hand. "I don't think any of that at all. I thought it was obvious that I'm proud of you for doing what gives you purpose. I'm the last person to tell someone they're wrong for chasing after an unconventional path. If I could, I'd stand on a different corner of LA every day holding up a sign that tells others to follow their hearts too."

She grips my hand back and relaxes in her seat.

"Teddy's proud too, but he's also your big brother. He just cares about what's best for you." I gulp and pull my hand back to my side of the table, very aware that what I just said is the very opposite of me.

I'm no good for her.

She traces the tip of her finger along the menu as her lips curl and fall, then curl up again in a small smile that peeks through her contemplative expression like a budding flower from a thick bush. "Thank you."

We share a deep but flitting moment of unique understanding. It feels strangely intimate, and we're not even fucking touching each other. What is up with me this week?

"Besides, Teddy has no room to criticize." I smirk, breaking the trance that temporarily suspended us in an odd but terrifyingly satisfying moment.

She lurches forward. "Right?"

"I tell him all the time to make better choices, but he thinks he has his shit together all because he has a monotonous fucking job in real estate." I shake my head as the server sets down a couple of shrimp baskets on the table next to us.

And my stomach growls yet again as the smells of fried breading and lemon wafts over me along with the salty breeze.

"The guy sleeps with divorced mothers of twenty-something-year-olds like that's where his commission comes from," I continue, trying damn hard to stop staring—and drooling—at the shrimp.

But when Sam gasps, it's easy to focus back on her. She

always has an adorable set of reactions that make her eyes light up, a twinkle of mischief and intrigue in them. Right now, there's also a hint of shock as she asks, "You don't think it does, do you?"

I squirm on my stool and only manage a snort. Besides, there's no way Teddy's getting paid for *those* kinds of services.

"I'm serious. This Bianca woman is the third cougar he's slept with this year. Has he been seeing anyone who's our age?" she presses, entertaining the ridiculous idea with animated intrigue in her eyes.

"Not that I know of…"

Our server returns and sets our drinks in front of us, after which she jots down our food order and then disappears.

"We'll dissect your brother's issues later when he's here to defend—and explain—himself." I interlock my fingers together. "When are you going to turn your phone on?"

"I'm not ready." She runs her fingers over the edges of her phone, the dark screen putting off a real doom-and-gloom vibe.

"You have to do it at some point."

"Oh, I didn't realize I couldn't just hide forever." She looks up and twists her lips into a seemingly uncomfortable grimace.

"I'm trying to help." I lean forward. "We agreed this morning that we'd start enjoying this island for real, which means taking care of the thing that's holding you back. It's not going to be fun here if you keep using it as a hiding place."

She blows out a frustrated breath.

"Be free," I urge Sam and hold my drink up.

"I'll check it when we're back in our rooms."

"Or you could check it now while I'm here. For support, of course."

"You're just nosy."

I scratch the back of my head and squint at the sun high in the sky, then drop my gaze to meet hers. "All shit aside, I really do want to help. If you don't want to face the wrath yet, it's your decision, but I think it would be good for *you*. Not me or anyone else, for that matter. Honest truth." I place my hand over my chest, which tightens under my palm as I realize this is the most sincere I've ever been with a woman.

Sam and I might've known each other for a while, but we've rarely hung out alone long enough to dig deep into our damn souls like this.

How does she do that?

Maybe it's because she's honest with me too—that has to be it. I'm just returning the sentiment, is all. She doesn't have magical powers or anything like that.

We're just good friends, and that's the only reason I'm so invested in convincing her to enjoy herself.

It has nothing to do with the fact that it makes me feel damn good to make her smile.

Sam chews the inside of her cheek, and her expression is somewhere between amused and scared. After a brief pause, she picks up her phone and sighs again. "Fine. Let's see the fucking damage."

I scoot my stool around the table for a better view as she switches off the airplane mode, and the impending notifications filter in, one after another. They appear so quickly that they make my head spin.

"Jesus," I mutter.

"This is what I was trying to avoid." As she slumps over the table, her body—even her soul, it seems—shrinks right next to me, and it guts me. "Shit."

I peer at the message she points to in her texts—Jason. "What does that prick need twenty-seven messages to say? Christ."

"I can't imagine it's anything good." She clicks on the

messages, one at a time, and most of the recent texts only ask if she's receiving them.

Using all caps.

"Oh my God. This one." She points at one of the first messages, where he apologizes for the breakup but says he doesn't want to be tied to a social media "piranha." It's obvious he meant pariah. "He can't even get the right freaking word."

"It might've been autocorrect," I blurt.

"Whose side are you on?" she snaps.

"Yours." I lean back, hands up. "He's an idiot. You're beautiful. Better?"

"Yes." She wiggles on her stool, and a small smile plays on her lips as she scrolls through more of Jason's messages, each one nastier than the last.

One calls her a bitch.

Another says she's a selfish attention whore.

My blood boils with every hurtful word thrown at her.

Where the hell does he get off talking to a woman—especially someone as good as Sam—like that?

"Fuck this douchebag. Let me at him." I reach for her phone, ready to rip him a new one with insults locked and loaded like a cannon.

Puny calves.

Even punier brain.

I have plenty at the tip of my fingers, but she holds her phone out of my reach and shakes her head. "Wait your turn," she grinds out. "How dare he." She slams her phone down, her cheeks flushed and redder than the sunburn on her shoulders.

At the table next to us, the pair drops their shrimp and glances in our direction, and I offer them a smile before I lean into Sam. "I'm sorry I asked you to open these here. This requires the walls of one of our private rooms where you can scream and throw shit. Want to get our food to go?"

"Definitely. And a pitcher of skinny margaritas with plenty of tequila."

"On it." I tap my knuckles on the table—if only I could flip it over in her honor.

Who the fuck does Jason *Douche* think he is, saying that shit to Sam? She's one of the best people I know and doesn't deserve to be treated like anything less.

Rage pricks my nerves as I find our server inside by the register and tell her our change of plans, followed by an apology for the abrupt request. From the way she exhales in relief, I'd say we did her a favor, though. The place is packed, and she obviously has her hands full—we're one less table she needs to worry about.

Once everything is boxed up and sealed, I check out, leaving her a hefty tip.

Sam joins me at the front and takes a bag, freeing my hand, which I place on the small of her back as we exit the little shack.

"I invested so much time in Jason. What was I thinking? I based a chunk of my business on a relationship that wasn't even going anywhere." Sam frowns. "What am I supposed to do with all my merchandise? I literally have an entire line of apparel centered around this whole idea of a mysterious boyfriend."

"You didn't know it wouldn't lead anywhere."

"Over the last week, I've started to feel like I did. Part of me always knew, and I should've ended things before they ever began." She waves her free arm up and down over her body, the flimsy tank top she wears over her swimsuit rising as we walk. "Besides, have you seen or heard me cry over him? He's the longest relationship I've ever been in. I should've cried at least once."

Although I get her point, I don't outwardly agree with her since I'm selfishly happy she's not wasting tears on that fucker.

"It's hard to cry on this island." I spread my arms out and

use the bottle of margarita from the café to point at the palm trees.

She comes to an abrupt stop, whirling toward me. "If he meant anything to me like I once thought, I would've cried. Not even watching the most brilliant sunset from the beach with a glass of rosé in my hand would've stopped me."

I sigh. "If you ask me, you're more upset by the backlash of the viral video than the breakup with Jason, which says a lot. And it's a good thing you're not together anymore, but it's not okay for him to talk to you like he did in those texts."

"Oh, he'll pay for that. But what do I do about my business? What the hell am I supposed to do now? If I don't come up with something seriously inspiring, funny, and mind-blowing, I'm going to take a hit larger than if a meteor struck me down right this second."

My laugh bursts out of me before I can stop it, but I choke it down once her glare bores into me. "What? That was funny," I mutter as I jog to catch up to her.

We resume our short walk toward the hotel, but our steps are much slower than they were on the way to the beach earlier.

"I sell so much merchandise with the logo *hashtag Gym Bae.* Not just more than I expected, but it's enough to cover my rent and then some. My followers are obsessed with the mystery of who it could be. From what I've gathered from those remaining online and interested, they're guessing it's Jason since he's in the video. Most don't know who he is and are disappointed it's not a movie star like Ian Brock, or someone of that caliber. Why they think I have connections to Hollywood stars is beyond me." She laughs, but it's sad. "Others are giddy no matter what, but some are *hashtag Team Jason.* The latter really fucking stings."

We reach our hotel with plenty of daylight left, and I rack my brain for a solution to her issue. Anything to show people who he really is—an asshole.

And who she really is—a light in the world of social media.

I'd do anything to help Sam get back to the glow she had while sitting in the hammock last night. The laugh she lets loose when Teddy and I tell her how gross vegetables are.

The spark in her spirit when she's at the gym.

I've watched many of her videos online, and even through the camera lens, I can tell it's more than a job to her. Her career cannot end this way.

In my room, she tosses her beach tote onto the couch and paces. "I know I can't make everyone happy, but this feels like I've duped my followers, which many have pointed out already. Some even cut up their shirts to show their disapproval, and I haven't even confirmed or denied anything." She wraps her arms around her midsection. "I just wish there was something I could do to turn this around. Save face. Show them I'm not a greedy manipulator who's simply after sales and followers. I mean, it was supposed to be for fun, and one innocent mistake just threw the whole thing—"

"Say it's me," I blurt, blinking rapidly.

What the hell did I just say?

"What?" She stops and faces me, her expression blank.

I quickly run through a mental flow chart, placing the pieces of this insane puzzle together like I rearrange Post-It notes on the wall when I'm trying to flesh out a plot.

But if it'll help Sam—and I think it will—I'll do it.

"Tell them you and Jason were just friends from the fitness industry, but any connection has been severed in light of recent events. The real mystery guy is me."

"How is that better? I'd still be lying."

"Or it's a friend"—I point to myself, then her—"getting another friend out of trouble. This is your business. Your reputation. You shouldn't get burned because of asshat *Douche*."

She worries her bottom lip between her teeth, tugging and

pulling with hesitation as she paces in front of the bed again. On top of the floral bedspread are bags of clothes from the hotel gift shop. Each item is a bright color, and they all spill out of the bags in chaos, which is how I feel.

If she goes along with this idea, we'd be unleashing a hell of a lot of chaos—a mess that's not easily cleaned up.

I need to call this off. Tell her I'm kidding. Brainstorm other ways to fix her situation.

But instead of being rational, what do I do? I step toward her and grab her hand like I'm asking her to fucking marry me. "Hear me out. I'm best friends with your brother, so you didn't want to out us until you knew we were serious, which as far as they need to know, we are. Take it from me, people fucking love their forbidden and taboo romances. They'll eat this shit up."

"What about Teddy, though? He'll see all of this."

I grimace, recalling his promise to cut off my favorite body part. "We'll tell him the truth and explain the plan. He can't get mad if our relationship is fake and strictly an online show. It's perfect."

She crosses her arms over her tantalizing chest. "And what's in it for you?"

"It would honestly boost my own stock, so to speak." I shrug, but inside, my heart is two stupid comments away from leaping out of my chest. "I could use any extra publicity before we start filming in the fall, and I hear you have quite the following." I wink and internally pat myself on the back for thinking on my feet so quickly.

I've trained my creative muse well after years of practice in the writing room.

"It's an audience built on fitness," she points out as if it's news to me.

"So? They still watch TV, don't they? You do."

She nods, sinks her teeth into her lip some more, then squints at me. "We'll use each other, then?"

"Not use. *Help*." I grip both her arms and slide my palms up and down them. "It's a win-win."

Small trails of salt still line parts of her tan skin, even though we rinsed off before we left the beach. Her tank top is hiked up above the waistband of her cut-off shorts, revealing a sliver of golden skin. She's every wild fantasy, which is probably the reason I say what I do next.

"Even if I don't get anything in return, I'm still happy to do whatever you need," I rasp.

Her lips part.

"I could use the public boost, but seriously, I got lucky and walked away from the Zoey mess unscathed. Let's be honest—I had nothing to really worry about it in the first place. Everyone in Hollywood is sleeping with each other." I laugh, but it's soft and nervous. Why am I sweating? And why the fuck am I trying so hard to convince her to do this? "Let me share my good fortune."

"If you want to do some good to earn that luck, buy yourself a Prius." She snorts.

"Whoa." I hold my hands out. "That's even crazier than this idea."

"So you admit pretending to date is crazy?"

"Of course, it is. This trip was crazy too, but look how it turned out." I squeeze Sam's shoulders and turn her toward the tropical view outside my sliding door, then whisper in her ear, "What do you say?"

Her frown transforms into a smile, and she leaps into my arms, squealing. "Let's do it! Thank you, thank you, thank you."

I squeeze my arms around her narrow waist, enjoying her seductive scent of salt and summer wrapped in one ball of energy. Then I set her down on her feet and put some distance between us before I get too overwhelmed by the perfect way she fits into my embrace.

Pretend.

We're now friends who are pretending to be a couple—all for show.

I rub my hands together and ask, "What's the first step?"

"Pictures, of course. The backbone of social media." She pulls her phone out of the back pocket of her scant shorts and snaps her fingers. "Oh, and I do need to address the incident. I'll forego the explanation and just give a quick apology for not doing my due diligence. Then I'll follow it up with pictures of you and me. Hopefully, they'll be so excited by our... deep and meaningful love story... they'll forget the whole humiliating thing."

I laugh. "You're an evil genius."

"Not evil. *Smart.*" She shrugs, sticking her tongue out. Pointing to the sliding door that leads to our adjoined patios, she tilts her head. "Natural sunlight is the best for pictures, and I want our grand announcement to be epic."

"Wow. Dating you is going to be exhausting, isn't it? What with constantly looking good and everything." I pat my hair down in exaggeration.

She crosses the room and squeezes my hand, bringing her lips only an inch from mine. It jolts my body to attention, hard and humming.

"Good thing we're not dating." Her cheeks split open into a wide grin, and in a blink, she yanks my arm to lead me outside. With her fingers near the handle, she stops and lets go of my hand to grab the leis from the desk.

I catch my breath as I follow her bouncing form, asking myself one question over and over again with each hurried step.

Is this a good idea?

I don't fucking think so.

Chapter 8
SAMANTHA

It's a crazy idea, risky and reckless, and I should not be putting my reputation on the line like this. Then again, my reputation sucks harder than a fucking tick right now, so what do I have to lose?

Besides, it's not a half-bad idea. It doesn't matter that Xander was blowing smoke up my ass earlier—he was right. People love forbidden and taboo romances, and dating my brother's best friend is definitely that.

Some have unfollowed me and continue to make memes, but I still have plenty of people waiting with an open mind for an explanation. One that will smooth things over. The sooner that happens, the faster we can get back to building an uplifting community.

After all, that's what my business is about. It has nothing to do with my personal love life, so this little white lie will just refocus my brand on the things that truly matter.

As for Teddy, I'll need to figure out what to tell him, but it should be easy, right? I come up with content regularly for my platform, subtly encouraging my followers to buy something—

clothes, swimwear, supplements, the idea of a healthy and balanced lifestyle—without shoving it in their faces.

I can convince my own brother that this is a good and innocent ruse.

With leis draped around both of our necks, I drag Xander through the sliding glass door, and the cool air of the room is quickly replaced by the afternoon heat. Hand in hand, we walk between the orange-cushioned chairs, the glittering path in a staggering pattern behind us. The shiny stepping-stones are nestled between grass and lead us through the gate, which is lined with meticulously kept bushes of hibiscus. The deep pink of the flowers pops against their green backdrop of leaves. I've spent a lot of time staring at the blooms since we arrived.

I just wish I could dig up a bush and take it home with me. If I ever actually decide to leave this paradise, that is.

Once our bare feet hit the grass, I turn on the camera, hold it above my head, and twist and turn until I get the angle right. The sun is high right now, casting a shadow on us from where I hold my phone, so I move it lower until we no longer have rectangular dark patches across half our faces.

"One thing." I move toward the gate that comes up to my waist and unlatch it, leaving it halfway open in hopes that it looks more whimsical in the picture this way—the small details matter, after all.

"Ready?" I ask Xander, dancing into place with my camera held high once again.

I watch him on the screen as I loop my arm through his, ready to act my ass off, but he obviously isn't. His expression is more uncomfortable than if he were wearing pants three sizes too small.

"Could you be frowning any harder?" I nudge him with my shoulder. "If we're going to sell this, you need to smile. And get closer to me."

"I'm used to being the one behind the scenes with a script, not in front of the camera," he mumbles, his low voice washing over me and weakening my knees.

I turn my head toward him, but the second I notice how very close his lips are to mine, my cheeky response gets caught in my throat before it can roll off my tongue.

His own tongue peeks out to lick his bottom lip.

He flicks his gaze down to my mouth and back up to my eyes, heat rolling off him like he himself is the sun.

My throat dries, especially when he gives me a smolder not even nuns could resist. "How's this?" he whispers, his minty breath brushing against my mouth.

It's enticing.

"Fine," I manage, my voice cracking.

I swallow, dangerously close to calling this whole thing off, but force a smile, instead. It's something I've grown accustomed to. When I'm too stressed or distracted to take a decent picture, my trick is to think of all the things that make me happy—flowers, hiking, a new shaker cup. It gets a natural grin out of me every time, and it works now too.

Xander follows my lead, and we both look into the camera. I snap a few shots as we get more comfortable, until we're full-on smiling and laughing. Even without inspecting each image, I know there are a lot of good ones, especially with the waving branches of palm trees in the background.

As sweat trickles down our backs from the warm afternoon, I instinctively lean into him, melting against him so perfectly that I briefly wonder how two people could fit this well.

I'm hot, but I can't get close enough to him.

My body involuntarily responds to his muscled arm around my waist.

My side tingles as his fingers grip my bare skin where my

tank has ridden up—and it rides higher the more we change poses, varying from staged to candid.

The longer I press my breasts against him, the more my skin burns.

Surprising shivers of… something… shoot down to my core.

And Xander kisses my cheek.

His mouth is on me, and I happen to take a picture at the exact moment his lips meet the corner of mine.

My sharp inhale echoes between us.

All thoughts escape me, and the island ceases to exist.

He licks his lips again like he did before I snapped the first shot, and I drop my arm that holds the phone, my chest heaving.

It's the same look he gave me while we were swimming.

When his rugged hands were on me.

A soft breeze caresses my cheek, but it does nothing to cool me off.

I close my eyes as Xander closes the little distance between us and crushes his lips to mine in a kiss so unexpected and passionate, my knees buckle.

Immediately, I press myself flush against him and tangle my tongue with his like we know this dance already, even though we've never kissed before.

I've never been kissed by anyone like this before.

It's electric.

Heady.

He kisses me with fervor like it's his last minute on earth, and it sends my nerves into overdrive.

He fists my hair, his grip firm and confident, and I gasp into his mouth, tugging on his T-shirt. I pull it over his head, breaking the kiss for mere seconds. Once the shirt is tossed to the side, he covers my mouth with his again and slips his skilled tongue between my already swollen lips, drinking me in.

Sucking.

Teasing.

It's a precursor to the things he would do to me if we were both completely naked, and I want to experience it.

I've never been more certain of anything.

"God," I breathe, deepening our kiss further, and he meets me in the middle with urgency, sliding his hands down the column of my neck and over my shoulders, until he reaches my hips.

He digs his fingers into my skin and hoists me up, pushing my back against the closed sliding glass door. I wrap my legs around him and squeeze, never interrupting our kiss, which turns messy.

Wild.

Taunting.

I'm so lost in it that I don't realize Xander moves his hand from my hip to the door and opens it.

Once we're inside, the cool air of the AC hits my slick skin, and I moan—loudly.

It seems to spur him on, because Xander spins us in place until my back slams against the wall and rattles the flower painting by the lamp. Our movements grow more hurried. More heat flashes down my spine, and my hands dive into his hair, roughly tugging him to stay close as he claws at my clothes.

Anticipation pools in my center, and our combined pants are in sync like joined hands.

I want him.

Now.

The lamp falls, and the crash echoes somewhere in the distance. It's too muffled by our needy explosion of lust, grunts, and whimpers as the salty remnants of the ocean on my body mix with his.

I bump into the office chair, and Xander rolls it aside with one hand, then props me up onto the desk, his movements chaotic and jerky.

He's so unlike himself—more feral and intense than I've ever seen him.

His touch is new and exciting, and welcomed too.

I scoot to the edge of the desk, pulling at the string on his shorts, and he uses his tongue to trace a line up the column of my neck like he's taking a hit of a drug.

Then he deeply inhales as if to savor me, which urges me to move faster.

I yank on my shorts, along with my bikini bottoms, until they're both hanging off one ankle, while Xander shoves his swim trunks down and holds a finger up, his eyes darting around the room. "I need... Hang on."

I bite my lip and nod frantically as if this is the most important moment of our lives. While I kick my bottoms the rest of the way off, he grabs a condom from his wallet and rips it open with his teeth, his dark hair falling over his forehead as he sheaths himself.

God, he's thick and ready—as am I.

The high-pitched calls of the birds outside sound through the open door as he stalks toward me with purpose and settles between my widespread legs. With one swift motion, he thrusts into me, knocking my head backward against the wall.

"Yes... God, yes," I sputter as I cling to his shoulders harder than I do a bar during a pull-up.

As he pumps into me, I run my hands under his loose tank and along the grooves of his back, losing myself in Xander Logan.

He's rough, yet tender.

He nuzzles his nose into the crook of my neck, and his heavy pants are hot on my shoulder.

I fight for breath as we continue rocking into each other, the tension building as the smell of sex and summer fills the room. The white-and-yellow leis are still draped between us, rubbing together with every roll of his hips.

It's not long before petals come loose and fall from the leis, sprinkling specks of color around us.

"Ah!" I cry, my mouth hanging open as he changes his angle and reaches my sweet spot.

The spot deep inside me that makes me forget my damn name—he found it like he already knew exactly where to look.

His grip around my waist tightens as he lets out a strained sound of his own that's a grunt, groan, and cry all in one. I barely even register it as I shudder in his arms, taking him with me as we both find release.

Sweat beads down his forehead, and I struggle to swallow around the lump in my throat.

Still clinging to him, I dip my head and let out a soft laugh, my chest heaving. He drops his chin onto my shoulder, and he laughs too as we ride out the blissful aftermath of our climaxes.

I open my mouth to say something, but I'm interrupted by a deep groan.

"Hmm?" I blink until the messy room comes back into focus.

Another grunt sounds, but it's higher pitched than before. I tilt my head to the side, and something moves in my periphery by the sliding door.

I turn in that direction to find... a pig?

Shrieking, I try to jump, but Xander's body is still holding me down. I kick my legs out, and he throws himself on top of me on the desk.

The squealing baby pig races behind Xander, swaying from side to side like it's drunk.

"Oh my God!"

"What the fuck?" Xander scrambles away from me,

bumping into the corner of the bed as the pig turns in circles in the kitchenette, his oinks loud and frantic.

I cover my mouth and curl my legs up to climb the rest of the way onto the desk.

"It's okay. It's okay." Xander holds his arms out to me, his attention trained on the animal, which is running around the kitchen like a bull at a rodeo. "It's harmless. It's just scared."

I nod, clutching my chest.

Xander inches toward me and gently touches my arm, then tilts his head toward my legs. "You, um... Your shorts are still..."

I glance down and instantly realize I'm still half-naked, and my bare ass is leaving an imprint on the desk. "Oh, God." My heart rate picks back up as I hurry to cover myself.

I can hardly think straight enough to button my shorts, and my trembling fingers from satisfaction and adrenaline are not helping.

Xander secures his shorts in place too, then helps me off the desk, muttering, "Gate was left open."

"Oh" is all I can manage.

"What do we do?" I ask, staring at the pig. Its perky ears stick straight up, and its squinty eyes peer over at us like it's trying to recognize us. "It's so scared."

I start to walk toward it, but Xander stops me. "Don't. I've heard that wild pigs around here are rarely ever friendly."

I bite my lip, running my hands down my shorts and peering over Xander's shoulder at the pig. "It's so tiny."

He hums, tiptoeing toward the phone. "I'm going to call down to the front desk for assistance."

I nod, frozen in place while the small animal and I have a staring contest.

But it doesn't last long.

The minute Xander hangs up after telling the staff of the situation, the pig rears its head back and charges at us.

I shriek again, and Xander grabs my arm, pulling me onto the bed next to him while the pig changes course and races into the bathroom.

Once it's quiet again, I lift what's left of my lei. "I guess we're going to need new ones."

He squeezes his arm around me and chuckles.

This is how animal control finds us—me wrapped in Xander's sculpted arms, my cheeks flushed, and not from the sun.

But because he and I just had sex.

On Maui.

Less than an hour after we agreed to *fake* date.

Nothing about the way he owned my body was fake, though. What am I supposed to do with that?

Chapter 9
XANDER

"You don't need to do all this—it's too much," Sam says as we follow the speed-walking hotel manager to one of their deluxe suites.

"We insist," she calls over her shoulder, waving her shiny key in the air.

I wipe my damp palms down the sides of my shorts, my nerves in overdrive, and not because of the rogue hog.

Or because Teddy's going to actually fucking kill me—although I don't feel great about that, either.

It's because the hotel staff is so apologetic over the pig running through our room that they want to upgrade Sam and me to their best available suite, free of charge.

As in, they're putting us in the same damn room.

I'm supposed to sleep in the same space as the woman I just fucked on a desk like a caveman.

My best friend's sister, at that.

I'm definitely not going to live to see my thirties.

They gave us complimentary drinks at the bar downstairs too, while we waited for them to get the place ready for us. Now we're buzzed, but it's still not enough to dull the feel of her eager fingers digging into my back or the sweet and salty taste of her on my tongue.

I run my hands through my hair, grains of sand still coating my head.

I never showered.

We went straight from lunch to sex to rescuing a pig, then watching the sunset while we drank our free cocktails.

I'm still covered in Sam, and our whole situation is making me dizzy.

"Here we are," the manager sings and opens the double doors, leading us to an extravagant room with an open floor plan and cream furniture.

Orange pillows fluffed on the couch brighten the sitting room, and several vases of fresh pink-and-white hibiscus flowers rest on the coffee table and kitchen counter. As we take the three steps down into the main room, my jaw drops—it feels like I just walked into a Hawaiian magazine. There's even an infinity pool beyond the sliding glass door. Next to the shimmering water is a small deck surrounded by a balcony that overlooks the beach.

"The fridge is stocked with waters, snacks, and other drinks. Chilled champagne is outside and ready for you as well."

"While we really appreciate this, it's too much. We can't possibly stay here." I shake my head, backing away as guilt settles on my chest.

I'm being handed the fucking lottery, but I don't deserve it. Not after what I just did.

"Nonsense. We take care of our guests around here like they're family, and we can't apologize enough for the inconvenience." The manager outstretches her hand toward the balcony. "At least no wild animals can reach you up here."

Sam dips her head and giggles, and I can't help myself, either.

Is it possible that's why the hotel had two available rooms on the ground floor when we first arrived? It is a popular time of year to visit the island, but it seems the other guests knew the risks of sleeping where mischievous pigs could play pranks on them.

I'll be locking away that piece of intel for future reference, just in case.

"I'll leave you to it. If you have any questions or need anything at all, please don't hesitate to reach out." The manager smiles at both of us and nods. "Aloha."

Once we're alone in this massive suite—wearing new leis that the hostess downstairs gifted us—I idly rub my chest over my bright yellow shirt and follow Sam toward the bedrooms. There's one on either end of the suite, far from each other, so that eases some of my nerves. It's much like the adjoining rooms we just had, so I can easily stay on my own side.

No big deal.

After we're done exploring, we make our way onto the balcony, still too stunned to speak. The sun has started setting, and the colorful glow is reflected over the water, forming a Christmas-tree shape along the surface. A bottle of champagne is nestled in an ice bucket on a small table between two chairs, just like we were told.

It's all very... romantic.

And on top of that, Sam and I are very alone for the first time since we ripped each other's pants off.

I tighten my jaw as the weight of the afternoon comes crashing down on me. "Well, I wanted us to enjoy the island, but the pig was a bit much." I chuckle, strolling toward the champagne.

"I'm going to have nightmares." Sam wraps her arms around her midsection. "I mean, I didn't eat bacon much before this trip, but I definitely won't be eating it now." She snaps her gaze at me and says, "I know we added pig roast to our list, but there's not a chance in Hell I can do that now. Not after Albert barreled into our lives."

I fight another chuckle when she says the name she gave the pig while we were at the bar. We were surrounded by other people, and it was far easier to give the pig a silly name than it was to address the elephant in the room.

The very heavy elephant between us.

"I'm with you," I offer. "If I saw all my food alive and well before I ate it, I'd become a vegetarian so fast it'd give me whiplash."

"I'm one veggie burger away from being a vegetarian. I should just make the leap."

"You and your principles." My eyes travel over her lean figure in admiration of her dedication.

I may not always agree with it, but I respect the hell out of her for it. It's paid off over the last few years—in more ways than one.

It was stupid fucking hot to have those long legs squeezed around my waist earlier...

She catches me staring and shifts from one foot to the other as the energy around us thickens.

Sam frees her wavy hair from a ruffled scrunchy and tousles it over her shoulder with a giggle, but it sounds nervous. "I didn't take a good look at the bathroom, but how much do you want to bet it's encrusted with gold?"

"I'd bet my vintage typewriter on it."

Her smile eases and becomes more genuine, but then she scrunches her nose. "I'm overdue for a shower."

"Like a library book." I blow out a frustrated breath and grip the back of my neck. "Wow. That sucked. I'm sorry."

"No, no." She waves. "I'm the one who's sorry you're using your best stuff on me. Save *something* for your scripts."

"Ha. Ha." I lift an eyebrow and shift on my heels. *Here goes nothing...* "Listen, about earlier—"

"We don't have to talk about it." She shrugs. "It was silly."

"I'm so glad you said that." Wincing, I jolt toward her. "I mean, it was great. You... Sam, you're amazing, but it was so reckless."

"Right." She nods, waving her arm toward the breathtaking view, and rationalizes, "Besides, it's not our fault. We're in a romantic place and just got carried away, but it was very reckless, for sure. Too complicated. Totally agree."

"Exactly." I work my jaw back and forth as our eyes lock. "We can go back to normal now. It'll be like the three-second rule, where no one needs to know we dropped food on the floor and ate it."

Her lips twist. "That's not scientifically accurate, nor did you just drop your dick inside me for only three seconds."

I let out a rough exhale, my stomach in fucking knots. "That's not what I meant—it was just an analogy, which you... hate."

Could I be any more of an ass right now?

"Like I said, we don't have to talk about it." She sways to the side and hooks her thumb over her shoulder. "I'm going to shower."

Guilt eats away at me as I watch her slink toward the sliding door. When her fingers curl around the handle, I swipe at my lips and raise my voice when I say, "It doesn't change anything with our deal, though."

"What?"

"I meant what I said earlier. I'll do whatever you need me to, including being your online boyfriend.

Her expression softens. "Thank you. That means a lot."

With a tight-lipped smile, I walk over and lean around her shoulder to open the door for her. As I do, I breathe in her sweet smell, and I have to suppress a deep-rooted groan, especially when she works her bottom lip between her teeth.

The same lip I spent much of the afternoon kissing.

And now, we've decided not to pursue whatever this is between us.

The click of the door behind her is deafening, and I'm not sure how long I stare at it before I finally force myself into one of the cushioned chairs and sip straight from the champagne bottle.

It's for the best—I know this deep down—but it doesn't stop me from being so damn disappointed.

The next morning, I stand in front of Sam's bedroom door, two gourmet coffees in hand from the fancy machine in the kitchen, and I deeply inhale like I'm about to pitch a new movie idea to the Hollywood gods.

All I could do last night was think of Sam.

Her tan skin against mine.

Her round ass in my hands.

The sounds she made while I drove into her with uncontrolled need.

She enjoyed it as much as I did.

But as I told her and myself last night, it's for the best that we don't let this come between us. We can enjoy the luxury suite, finish the trip, and head back to reality, where we never speak of yesterday, especially to Teddy. I've never seen him throw a punch, but I'm positive he'd do a lot worse if he found out I slept with his sister.

Fuck.

Grinding my jaw, I knock on her door as best I can with the hot drinks in my hand, then catch movement in my periphery.

Sam leans against the wall, her arms crossed. Her headphones are wrapped around her neck, and her smug grin is more amused than Jack Nicholson's portrayal of the Joker.

"How long have you been standing there?" I grimace.

She pushes off the wall, and her grin widens with every step she takes toward me, her legs slick with sweat. Instead of it turning me off like it might for someone like Jason *Douche*, I'm fucking salivating like a dog.

She looks like she spent all morning rubbing oil on them.

"Long enough to place a bet with myself that it would take you seven whole minutes to knock on my door, and guess what? I won."

"All right, all right. You caught me." I laugh, but the sound quickly evaporates. When she looks at me, a shadow cast over her eyes, heat trickles down my body, and I fight the urge to adjust my pants. "I brought coffee." I shove one mug at her.

"Thanks." She accepts it as she brushes past me to open her door.

I'm frozen in place, catching a whiff of her body spray mixed with sweat. She's drenched from head to toe like she took a dive in the pool, but I know she simply works that hard whether she's in her home gym, the hotel fitness center, or outside.

I just never see it firsthand. In her videos, Sam lifts heavy weight, but she's usually so put together.

Right now, the damp *V* down the valley of her breasts shouldn't be sexy, but it is. It really fucking is when it's Sam.

"It's okay to come in. I'll keep my clothes on until after you leave." She juts her hip out as she places her headphones on the dresser.

A strangled, incoherent sound escapes me, and I attempt to cover it with a cough. *Get a grip, man.*

"What's up?" she asks, then takes a sip of coffee.

I cross the threshold into her room, noting the open suitcase in the corner that's exploding with different colored fabrics and lace—fucking hell, her thongs are strewn across the top like they're on display.

They scream *come hither.*

How am I not supposed to look?

Okay, okay, I'm not a horny fifteen-year-old. I can have a mature conversation with my *friend*—more importantly, *Teddy's sister.*

I rub my hands together, plastering a smile on my face like I did when Ronald would ignore my suggestions in the writing room—never show weakness. "We need to get moving if we're going to make our reservation."

"To eat? I was going to make oatmeal here this morning."

I shake my head. "We're going to find sea turtles."

She furrows her eyebrows.

"The list." I set my coffee down and tiptoe toward her like I'm walking on eggshells. I just don't trust myself, and I'm far too aware there's a neatly made bed next to us that needs to be ruffled up. I'm hanging on by a fucking thread, my body hardening with each inch of distance I close. "We need to finish the items on our list before we can leave the island," I manage.

She eyes me. "You still want to do everything on our list?"

"Of course." I shrug. "Don't you?"

"I do. I'm just surprised, is all. I half expected you to have left already."

"Without you?" I step back, frowning. What kind of guy does she think I am? "I wouldn't just leave you here, Sam."

"After yesterday..."

"No matter what happened between us, I'd never abandon you on an island. I know I don't have the best track record when it comes to women, but I'd never stoop that low, especially with you."

"We agreed not to talk about it, so I'm sorry I brought it up." She squares her shoulders. "Let's do the list. I need twenty minutes to eat and change."

I nod and slowly back away, my feet heavy and stubborn.

Swiping at the corners of my lips like it'll help get the sour taste out of my mouth, I disappear into my own room, my mind racing.

What the hell?

She thinks I'm an asshole, and although I'd like to lock us in her room until I convince her I'm not, how would I prove it?

All I've ever done is show her I'm an asshole. One who breaks into her hot tub with a random girl whose name I don't remember.

A guy who sleeps with young up-and-coming actresses just to kill time and get on my boss's nerves.

That's who I am, and she met me long enough ago to *know* so many ugly details and indiscretions of my past.

I've never been ashamed about any of it, though. I'm enjoying what's left of my twenties. But now, it all feels icky.

I shouldn't care what Sam thinks. We agreed that yesterday didn't happen. We're not together, no matter what she decides to post online for her own reasons.

Yet, I can't help the churning in my stomach that nags me to show her I can be a decent guy. One she respects and even... likes.

Chapter 10
SAMANTHA

Xander's been quiet all morning.

The only thing he's said since we left the room was that we'd be going to Maluaka Beach, aka Turtle Town, to snuba dive and search for sea turtles. I didn't know what he meant by snuba diving when he first mentioned it, but he explained it's the best of both worlds of snorkeling and scuba diving.

And I'm excited to try it for the first time.

We've let the windows of our rental car down, and the wind blows across our cheeks. The salt from the ocean below tangles in my hair too. Although I imagine the waves crash hard in bursts against the rocky shoreline in the winter months, the sea is calm this morning. The deep green vegetation pops in the daylight like a painting.

The scenery is idyllic. Breathtaking. Almost too beautiful to be real.

But I can't enjoy any of it because Xander's silence is bugging me.

Is he upset about what I said before we left? He can't possibly be offended that I joked about him leaving me here.

Right?

I didn't actually believe he would, but to be honest, I wouldn't have been surprised if he had. He compared us to the three-second rule; the man is capable of anything.

Teddy once told me Xander climbed out of a second-story window after he found out he'd been the woman's first. He was gone before she came out of the bathroom, and he never returned any of her calls.

Of all the douchey things Xander's done when it comes to women, that might be at the top, in my opinion.

In any case, a second-story window is much different than escaping an island, and I'm his best friend's sister. It makes sense that he'd have more decency with me, but again, he talked about what happened between us like we were discussing a new haircut.

That should be reason enough to put him out of my mind. I just wish I could forget the way it felt to be so intimate with him.

It was... unreal. Everything about yesterday afternoon was—right down to the interruption.

And I can't stop thinking about it. All night, I tossed and turned and fought my urge to run across our new suite to break down his door in order to convince him to join me in my bed.

When we come to a stop in an empty parking spot, my heart rate picks up with anticipation of this adventure. I turn to express as much to Xander, but he hops out without a word.

"Okay, then," I mutter sarcastically to myself as I open the door. Immediately, I'm enveloped by the warm day in a comforting hug like Maui knows I need it.

I follow Xander to the shop, where we're greeted by a chipper young woman with more energy than a baby dolphin. She hands us our gear and gives instructions on how the tour will work. At the end of her spiel, she checks the time on her smart watch and smiles. "You can board Island Bliss in just a few minutes. The sea awaits."

We both thank her, then make our way to the beach, where we undress down to our swimsuits, and I try not to stare.

My *friend's* muscled back tapers and disappears into his bright blue swim trunks, which hang low and show off the dimples just above his round backside. My freaking mouth waters.

What a magnificent body he has.

And to think—I had my legs wrapped around it less than twenty-four hours ago.

He still doesn't speak as I stuff our clothes into my tote bag, and we're joined by a few others, who talk in hushed tones.

"For someone who was excited to come out here today, you have a sad way of showing it." I stare pointedly at Xander.

"I'm just ready to get out there. Supposedly, this is the best time to catch a bunch of turtles. We might even come across some manta rays." He wiggles his eyebrows, and although it's not his usual upbeat tone, it puts me at ease.

Progress.

As we join the rest of the group and walk toward a white and blue excursion boat bobbing over the water with ease. The name Island Bliss scrolled along the side, and a rail stands across the front, at the end of which is an opening to board.

As the captain addresses the group, Xander stands so close to me that his breath cascades over my shoulder, cool against my taut skin.

My eyelids flutter, and I almost miss the opening lines. "Aloha, and welcome to Island Bliss," the captain bellows out. "And I don't just mean the boat, but beautiful Maui itself."

When it's time to board, Xander hops in before me, then surprises me by offering his hand.

And I don't hesitate to grab it.

It's an innocent gesture, but I like the feel of his palm against mine.

The firm hold on me is comforting, yet intense.

I lick my lips as we settle next to each other near the back by another couple.

The sway of the boat from the soft waves below us rocks me from side to side, and the adventure ahead becomes more real.

I'm about to go snuba diving on freaking Maui!

The giddy flutters in my stomach make me smile, and I breathe it all in as the captain proceeds to describe the two dive sites we'll be visiting today, followed by facts of the reef. Unlike the shoreline reef, the ones we'll be visiting farther out into the ocean aren't damaged by people trampling on them.

He continues describing what we'll see, along with safety details regarding sea turtles and rays we might come across, as we head out to sea.

At one point, he pauses as a group of dolphins pops up next to the boat and swims along with us. We all *ooh* and *ahh* over the animals, enjoying their carefree jumps like we're watching innocent kids play and giggle.

I didn't see this many dolphins during the week I spent in Bali for a fitness and wellness retreat. A few of the locals had said there are several different species of dolphins that are always spotted in the area, so we took a boat out to the deep sea. We only saw a couple of the adorable creatures swimming about, though.

The ones here are a lot less shy, I guess.

I'm captivated by them and the scenery, and the rest of the ride flies by until we drop anchor. Blue water surrounds us for miles, and in the distance, green mountains stand tall like they're on watch, protecting us.

"I'm already glad we're doing this," I say to Xander, grinning widely as one of the guides connects my hose to the air supply that'll remain on a raft above the water surface. This way, we can stay under a lot longer than if we were snorkeling.

Once we're finally in the water, Xander and I stay close, pointing out anything we find cool. The clusters of coral lining the jagged hills. The school of yellow fish. The big pink-and-white starfish stuck to the side of a rock.

After several minutes, I get lost in my mission to find a sea turtle, and when I turn back around, Xander is no longer next to me. I kick my flippers behind me to search for him, only to realize I've kicked him. I burst out of the water, my mask tight around my eyes and nose, and I yank the mouthpiece out, sputtering, "I didn't see you!"

"You did that on purpose," he calls out, raising his mask to wipe under his eyes.

When we dive back in, we're joined by a couple of green sea turtles, swimming gracefully like they don't have unexpected guests. My squeals are muffled underwater as I point them out to Xander, who's swam up beside me.

He dips deeper, swimming farther ahead, and I'm just about to follow when he abruptly changes course—as quickly as possible under water, that is. His mask makes it hard for me to read his expression, but when he gets close, I notice his eyes are wide and fearful. He waves me back up and grabs my arm when I don't move fast enough.

We emerge above water again, sputtering and breathing heavily. Instead of stopping, he grabs the raft and leads us back toward the boat while the rest of the group carries on.

"Everything all right?" the captain calls out and meets us at the edge of the boat.

Once we've climbed inside, I realize Xander's only wearing one flipper. "What happened to your—"

"The turtle... It bit my flipper... Just took it," he manages, trying to catch his breath as he rests his palms on both knees.

"A turtle?" the captain and I both repeat, stunned.

"I didn't think I was even that close—I know you said they're endangered, so I kept my distance—but one swam up fast and took me by surprise." Xander's chest rises and falls as he frantically nods, and then he confuses me further by bursting into hysterical laughter.

"That's not funny, *hoaloha*." The captain inspects Xander's ankle, and I look over his shoulder and find slight red lines marring his skin. "You're lucky they didn't take your whole foot with them."

Xander waves him off. "I'm fine. It's an experience, right? Who else gets their flipper stolen by a mean turtle?"

I cover my mouth, and I can't help my laugh, either. I'm still high on the epic excursion too. I mean, we just swam with turtles and other wildlife in the bluest water I've ever seen. Not to mention the pictures I snapped on the way here. The backdrop doesn't get better than this.

Given he's okay, how can I not laugh over the fact that my friend was just bullied out of his flipper by a turtle?

The captain, who's become a third wheel, shakes his head, leaving us alone on this side of the boat while the rest of the group finishes their swim.

Xander and I slide down to the bottom until our heads rest next to each other. We prop our feet up onto the seats along the sides, the swaying of the boat more prominent from this position.

"Can you believe that motherfucker?" he asks.

"I can believe something so ridiculous happened to you, yes." I shift closer to him. "You seem to attract a lot of angry animals. Should I be worried about hanging out with you?"

Laughter racks our bodies as we stare at the clear sky.

"That thing was scarier than if a megalodon had appeared

or if I'd somehow found myself in Themyscira with the Amazons."

I groan between giggles. "Either of those scenarios are more plausible than the day you admit you like egg whites."

"Or the day you admit you're bad at volleyball." His shoulder shakes against mine as he slaps a hand over his mouth like he didn't mean to say that—he knows I have a competitive edge.

"How dare you." I jerk up into a sitting position and shove him to the side. "I kicked your ass at beach volleyball, and you're just too stubborn to give me a compliment."

"I kept having to chase the ball into the water." He snorts, squeezing his eyes closed as I continue nudging him like I'm trying to throw him overboard.

Which isn't a bad idea.

"At one point, I thought I'd get carried away with the current all because you couldn't hit the ball on land even once," he continues goading me. "Tell me one thing—would it have been worth it?"

"As a matter of fact, yes," I joke, falling onto my back next to him again, the sun rays filling my skin and soul with Vitamin D.

"You're as cold as ice, I tell you." He clasps his fingers behind his head, his thick bicep tickling the edge of his ear. "Captain Rick mentioned these turtles can live into their eighties, sometimes even to a hundred. I think my nemesis was an old, cranky bastard."

"He's your nemesis now? You're not actually in a DC comic."

"What else am I supposed to call him when I tell this story to everyone I know? Harold?"

"Oh God, you're going to work a killer sea turtle into a screenplay, aren't you?" I roll my eyes.

It doesn't even matter what we're talking about. The most

important thing right now is that Xander and I are back to joking freely—the way we used to be.

It's easy and fun, and I'm thankful we're back to a good place, even if it took a sea creature nearly scarfing down his foot for lunch in order to get here.

I reach over to lift the weighted seat cushion and reach inside the hollow bench for my phone. After I fish it out of my bag, I hold it high and snap a few pictures of us.

I laugh into his shoulder, the ends of his damp hair tickling my forehead, while he murmurs about ridiculous plotlines he has in mind.

No matter what baggage we brought with us to this tropical island and how much we further complicated things yesterday, right now, we're just two people in paradise.

Normally, I've barely taken the picture before I swipe to Instagram, add my branded filter, and post along with a cheeky caption.

But right now, my first and loudest thought is to keep these images in a separate album as mementos. To look at them as proof that I'm alive and well and happy—with the one person who took me by surprise.

I'm in the moment, and Xander is making me realize how rarely I do that anymore. He's given me a new perspective on a lot of things, actually. For one, how unhealthy I've been in relationships, even before Jason.

Being on this trip with my friend has made me rethink what I want in a guy and how I should feel when I'm with one. How I should be free to be myself.

I might have ignored my phone for the beginning of this trip out of stubbornness and fear of humiliation, but the guy next to me has made it so much easier to enjoy myself.

Xander Logan is definitely a game changer.

Chapter 11
XANDER

As the sun sets, I'm still hyped on adrenaline from snuba diving, the turtle incident, and the drinks we had by the pool before we headed back to our room.

All is back to normal between Sam and me.

I only thought about her body against mine seven times today, which is impressive. Tomorrow, I know I can get it down to six, until eventually, I'm not thinking at all about how snugly my—

"See you tomorrow for hiking?" Sam asks, heading to her room.

I stop with my hand on the doorknob and turn to her, nodding. "Can't wait to see what derivative of a snack you'll bring with you," I toss back, recalling that she offered me dried pineapple chips earlier.

I know this island is practically made of pineapples, so I shouldn't be surprised that such a thing exists, but I was. Even worse was that she used the fruit's richness in fiber and enzymes, which are good for the digestive system, to convince me to eat it.

I ate a few of the damn rings just because of how adorable

she was while reciting the facts, and admittedly, they weren't half-bad.

"Just for that comment, I'll be sure to *accidentally* forget your peanut butter and jelly sandwich."

"In that case, I'll forget the bug spray."

She squints her eyes at me, obviously fighting a smile. "Well played, Logan."

I exaggeratedly take a bow.

She drops her hand from the door and points toward the sitting room. "I'm still pretty wired. Want to watch a movie or something?"

"You read my mind." I eye her bright expression, the tip of her nose tinted red. This island is a damn good look on her, and no matter what lines we crossed yesterday, I'm glad we're here together. "I just need to change first."

"Me too. My bikini has worked overtime this week, and it shows." She shimmies, and then in a fashion very unlike anything I'd expect from her, she pulls out a wedgie. "It had to happen."

I shake my head, laughing—and trying not to stare at her backside as she disappears.

Make that eight times.

Blowing out a frustrated breath, I enter my room, and even though a nice, hot shower sounds fan-fucking-tastic, a cold one would be smarter.

I'm overdue for a wise decision, so I deeply inhale as I step inside the freezing-cold tiled shower—which does not have gold flakes in it, by the way.

Sam's ridiculous.

And smart.

And damn sexy.

The way she whimpered while I held her in my arms was like music to my ears. The keys of a typewriter. The rainbow after rain.

Samantha Ray is unlike any woman I've ever met, and it took a trip halfway across the world to make me realize it.

Like I said, I'm not the smartest screenplay in the slush pile. Maybe that's why no self-respecting producer accepts any of my work.

"Fuck," I mutter.

This cold shower was supposed to help, but I'm harder than my sea turtle enemy's shell.

Clamping my chattering teeth down, I quickly dry off and throw on the electric-blue T-shirt I bought at the gift shop, along with the matching pants. The cashier insisted it was a set that could not be separated.

I really wish I had time to stop by my apartment before we flew out of LA like the apocalypse was coming, but then again, spontaneity is far more fun.

"Wow." Sam stands outside my door as I come out. "I was coming to see if you want popcorn, but now I'm wondering if you might like to strut your stuff first."

"I do, actually." I place both hands on my hips and take long strides toward the kitchen, exaggerating every movement and showing off my obscene Hawaiian pants. The floral design is obnoxious and worse than any shirt on a senior retiree.

Sam claps and cheers for me through her fit of snorts. "I seriously would've liked to be there when you bought those."

"They were the last pajamas in the shop," I explain. "Just wait until you see what I'm wearing on our hike tomorrow."

"Damn. Now I'm going to be up all night trying to guess what it is."

As Sam hops down the steps toward the couch, I can't help but stare at her swaying hips. It's obvious she was previously a model. Sam's beyond beautiful, with her large brown eyes, olive complexion, and long legs. She's also the perfect height for me to comfortably rest my chin on her head when we hug.

How did I not realize the latter before this week?

"What about *Forgetting Sarah Marshall*?" she calls over her shoulder as she scrolls through the guide on the TV.

"It's fitting." I toss a bag of complimentary popcorn into the microwave, then open the fridge to retrieve one of the cans from a six-pack I brought from our old room. "I'm having a beer. Want one?"

"I'll have a glass of the skinny margarita," she says, but her voice comes from right behind me, followed by the sound of a cabinet closing.

Holding a red cup in one hand, she reaches around me with the other for a tall yellow bottle, then pours herself a drink. After a sip, she asks, "Want to check out the posts I drafted this morning? One is me addressing and apologizing for the leggings situation, and the other is the big unveiling of my secret boyfriend's identity."

"Sure." The quick and loud popping sounds echo between us from the microwave as I face her, crossing my arms over the sunglasses-wearing pineapple cartoon across my shirt. "Have you heard from *Douche* any more?"

Sighing, she scrolls through her phone. "I sent him a single message to let him know I'm handling the situation and that I don't want to be tied to him, either. Let's just say, I made my dislike for him *very* clear."

Why does that make me deliriously happy? "Did he answer?" I ask carefully.

"He left me a voice message, which was hard to understand because of all the mumbling. He's not used to rejection, especially when he thought he was the one in control." She rolls her eyes, smug and content. "Fucking asshole."

"Won't argue there," I mumble and rock on my heels. I take

a sip of the cold beer in my hand and get lost in the slope of her shoulder.

The way she bites her lip on one side—it's always the left.

As she concentrates on the screen of her phone, she wiggles her toes too. It's a quirky tic of hers when she's nervous, and right now, I can relate, although my reaction is not from concern that these posts hold my future in their tiny, digital palms.

It's because I have to adjust myself and hope she doesn't look up in time to catch me in the act.

"Okay, here's the caption for the first post." She hands me her phone with an Instagram draft pulled up on the screen.

The microwave beeps between us, and a few kernels make sad pops as they give up with no more heat. As Sam reaches up to retrieve our evening snack, her shirt rides higher above the waistband of her cotton shorts, and I quickly drop my attention away from the torture and onto the phone screen.

Except that's torture in itself.

The image is the one I took of her in the hammock, where she wore a flowy dress the color of her pink nails. Her back is to the camera, highlighting the lean muscles there, and the palm trees stand tall on either side of her like props. She edited the picture with a filter and cropped the sides too, and it looks like it belongs in a magazine.

I tear my focus from it and scan the text, where she apologizes for her absence and for the incident itself. The rest of the caption makes jokes about being human, and at the end, she says she has a special announcement to stay tuned for.

Our relationship.

Even though I know it's fake, the thought makes my hard dick stir.

"It's good," I rasp and clear my throat. "Relatable and funny. People will respond well to it, and if they don't, they know where the unfollow button is."

She laughs into her handful of popcorn, and it makes me smile.

"Hey, you started without me," I tease. "Wait—you don't eat this shit. What gives?"

"I have cheat meals and snacks. I had my seafood pasta earlier, and now I'm having my dose of buttery goodness. Only a couple of handfuls, though." She passes me the bag and claps. "Okay, okay, I'm just going to post it. Why wait, right?"

"Exactly." I take another sip of beer and exchange her phone for the popcorn.

"It's done." She clutches the phone to her chest like it's a Bible as we walk to the couch.

"Relax." I sit next to her and pat her bare knee. "This is part of life in the limelight, isn't it? You have to deal with the occasional PR flop."

"I know, but it's hard to move on from the embarrassment. I mean, my ass is on the internet. My *ass*."

I grind my teeth, close to cracking a few molars as I attempt to tamp down the mental images of said ass. One I want to sink my fingers into again.

But I fucking can't.

"Let's watch the movie," I bite out more harshly than intended.

If she notices, she doesn't comment. Instead, she sets her phone facedown on the coffee table and settles her back into the cushions, which curve around her. This pillowy piece of furniture definitely passes the comfort test.

I could easily sleep on the damn thing if Sam weren't next to me.

Once she presses *Play* on the remote, she sips her drink, then licks her lips, all while I force myself to watch the movie instead of her.

Ten minutes in, my leg starts bouncing. I've never been so fucking tense.

Another ten minutes later, the smell of butter is long gone from the room, and she curls into a ball, tucking her feet underneath her. She stretches across most of the couch until her hair tickles my shoulder.

My body hardens.

And my leg stills.

The air around us is charged with intoxicating heat between us.

"I have a better idea." She stops the movie and nods out to the infinity pool. "Why don't we enjoy our drinks out there? We haven't christened it yet, and the water is calling to me."

"You haven't had enough? All we've done is swim." I chuckle, but it's strangled.

"We need to celebrate harder than this movie and popcorn." She jumps up, and her tits bounce along with her.

Wait... is she not wearing a fucking bra?

I gape as she skips to her room, extra enthusiasm in each step.

"Put your swimsuit on!" she calls out from behind the door, like she knows I haven't moved.

Does she know why, though? If she did, would she run back to her old room to get away from me?

Sam said our time together was impulsive. Spontaneous. A product of the island, like if we hadn't succumbed to its charm, it would've been disappointed.

She made it clear that's where we stand.

Just friends.

Besides, we had a good day, especially after the awkward morning we spent in silence. I don't want to risk ruining it by giving in to temptation a second time.

No matter how badly I want to.

Chapter 12
XANDER

While I change for our swim in the infinity pool, my tense jaw remains clenched through each movement, and my mind races with unappealing thoughts.

Birds.

Trees.

Socks.

Anything to get my stirring dick to calm down.

When I return to the main room, Sam is already outside and sitting on the edge of the pool, her feet dangling in the water.

Stepping through the open door, I ask, "What are we celebrating exactly?"

"Other than your win in the fight against your archnemesis?" She quirks a brow as she sips her margarita.

"I knew it would catch on." I smirk and step down into the water, then tilt my head toward her expectantly. "Well? What else are we celebrating?"

The smile she gives me is coy and a little shy. "My first post after a week. I don't think I've gone that long since I started my account."

"Seriously?"

Tousling her hair down her back, she hums like a tune is playing in her head and she wants to share it with me.

It's melodic and soothing.

It's too easy to get wrapped up in it—and her—especially when it's mixed with the soft breeze drifting through the palm trees below, producing a quiet song of its own.

Even though I'm in cool water, I'm on fire, so I dunk my head under in order to clear it.

When I come back up, I flick water at Sam, earning me a surprised squeal. "Are you just going to sit there, or get in? This was your idea, after all."

"All right, all right. No need to get violent." She wades into the pool until her shoulders are covered, and her red swimsuit lightens underneath the water, appearing pink, instead.

When she nears me, the water seems to get hotter, but I can't escape it. This pool is nowhere near as big as the one downstairs at this resort.

After swimming around each other for a few minutes, we drift to the edge for our drinks as her phone lights up next to her cup.

"What's the response been so far?" I ask over the top of my beer.

She swipes her finger along the screen. "Mixed. Some people say I'm only apologizing because my hands are tied, and it's not genuine—as I expected. But there's been an overwhelming number of supportive messages, comments, and shares, and that's what I'm going to focus on."

Sighing in contentment, she turns her phone over and leans her back against the edge.

There's a glow about her that wasn't there when we first arrived, and it fills my chest with gratitude and warmth. Even though there are still trolls out there trying to tear her down, she's choosing to focus on the important things. On the positive.

She's happy.

Before I realize it, I've inched toward her, standing a foot's length away, and her scent wraps itself around me.

The scenery—the world—it all fades.

"Are you sure you're still okay with pretending to be my boyfriend?" she asks. There's curiosity and fire in her eyes, like she wanted to ask me something else entirely.

All I can manage is a nod as my gaze settles on her lips.

The way her teeth graze the bottom one. Would I taste margarita on her tongue if I leaned in and captured her mouth with mine?

Would she arch her back for me again and give me more of those feminine whimpers I've been dizzy over?

"Post it now," I whisper, but the words are firm, as is the request.

Slowly, she reaches for her phone and taps on the screen a few times as Hawaiian music in the distance grows muffled by my heart thundering in my ears.

And blood rushes south.

"Done."

The word barely leaves her sinful lips before I grip the back of her neck and crash my mouth to hers.

She opens wide for me to taste more of her, and I indulge as if she were a tall glass of water on a hot day. I could get addicted to her taste as easily as a drug.

Sam matches each swipe of my tongue with her own and climbs up the front of me like a tree, her strong legs squeezing my waist.

Grunting, I grip her under both thighs and press her back to the side of the pool, my front flush against her slick body.

She's slippery, as is our kiss.

It's wet and heated and frantic.

I angle her head to the side and nip at her neck as she breathes my name in my ear, arousing me further.

The sweet and unique smell of her coconut lotion makes my mouth water, and even though she's showered and this isn't the ocean, I still lap up the faint taste of salt on her skin. Spending as much time as we have on the beach makes it seem like we'll never wash the bitter substance away.

I'll never be able to wash *her* away.

She's lit something inside me that was dull and mundane before we stepped off the plane a week ago.

And I want to bask in it—consequences be damned.

With new and determined urgency, I slide my hand into her sexy bikini top and cup her perky breast, the weight of it perfect in my palm.

She gasps, and her grip on my shoulders tightens, as do her legs around me. "More," she pleads. "Give me more, Xander."

"Whatever you want, gorgeous." I pepper kisses along her jawline, then dip my head chin deep below the water to pay special attention to her hard nipple.

My mouth covers the tight bud, and the small waves of the pool wash over my tongue as I lick and suck and nip. She gasps again, but it sounds more surprised than the first.

And I want to continue to catch her off guard. To have her writhing. To hear my name fall from her lips again.

I suck harder and gently bite down, reveling in the feel of her.

The taste of her.

What would it feel like if I tasted *all* of her?

I hoist her onto the edge of the pool and throw her legs open wide, which earns me the mother of all gasps.

"I want to make you come, Sam." I narrow my gaze at her,

and her chest expands at a rapid rate as she peers down at me through hazy eyes. "On my tongue."

I dive between her thighs, only one thing on my mind as I place a greedy kiss over her swimsuit.

I growl. "This bikini has been torturing me for days."

"Rip it. I don't care. Just... I need you." She leans down, bringing my face to meet her halfway for a searing kiss while I run my finger along the seam of her heat, the soaked fabric the only thing separating me from bliss.

Moving her dripping bikini bottoms aside, I break the kiss and dig in—literally.

I drag my tongue inside her folds, licking and sucking like I've been deprived of a woman's touch for years. And I might as well have been.

Nothing compares to Sam.

I continue my relentless feast, searching for her magical spot. Anything to make her feel good from my touch.

Fuck, I want to make her feel good.

To please and worship her.

I know I'm getting close when she spreads her legs even wider and clings to my hair in a strong, desperate grip.

"That's it. That's it." Her breaths are loud and sensual.

Hot and satisfying.

"Right there." She writhes beneath me, dragging her ass along the tiled edge.

She throws her head back as her climax pulses through her, ripping up and down her body, but she doesn't remove her hand from my hair. Instead, she twists a fistful of my strands like a squeeze toy.

And I welcome the sting.

Humming, I pull her back into the pool with me as I lick her taste from my lips and swipe at a stray line of her climax across my chin.

She's dazed and weak and doesn't immediately catch herself, but I grab her just before her head goes under the water. "Whoa," I say, my voice low.

"You, Xander Logan, have... moves." She swallows, and a slow smile teases her lips.

"Want to see my other moves?" I whisper in her ear, keeping her close.

Sam's bikini is in disarray, her cheeks are flushed, and thick strands of hair stick across her forehead. She's unraveled and so unlike her perfect pictures online.

And I couldn't want her more.

"Bring it." Her bottom lip trembles, which nearly knocks off a water droplet.

I lick it off myself as I cup her cheek in my palm and walk us backward until my ass hits the wall. We never break our kiss.

We massage each other's tongues while she reaches underwater and slides my shorts down.

As she climbs up the front of me, I sink farther into the warm pool and into a squatting position.

She brings her knees up on either side of me and deepens the kiss, her warm and wet mouth covering mine in a kiss so heady and exciting that I feel it in my whole fucking body.

Then she settles completely onto my lap.

And I do what I've been dying to do all day—I grab two fistfuls of her ass, kneading them and groaning with appreciation.

"Fuck me, Xander," she whispers, sliding against my aching dick, up and down in sync with the soft waves.

I squeeze tighter, her taste still lingering on my tongue, and the rest of my resolve crumbles, especially when she reaches a delicate hand between us and wraps it around my throbbing length.

"I have an IUD." She peers into my eyes. "And all my tests came back negative a couple months ago."

"Mine too," I manage, my favorite body part screaming in her hold.

Cupping my cheeks in her free hand, she surges upward and over, closing the distance between us and settling onto me with ease.

We both gasp at the initial jolt of relief and pleasure of me nestling myself deep inside her, thick and bare. The strong connection is mind-blowing and intense, and she must think so too because our mouths fall open at the same time.

Our lips barely touch.

It's like they're communicating on their own through breathy moans, and when our lips touch while we move, the spark from that small contact lights me on fire.

She starts slow as she rises up and falls down, her wet body sliding against mine with sexy precision. Then she rides me faster and wilder as my legs tense beneath her, holding us up with the help of the water.

"Fucking hell," I growl, and my teeth graze her chin.

It's not long before Sam is bouncing in my arms, and the splashes increase in size and sound. They mix with the beat of drums below, probably from a fun luau we're missing, but I don't give a shit.

There's literally nowhere else I'd rather be than here with Sam.

We continue splashing water more violently as she picks up her pace even more, and I meet her hips halfway, the friction of sex in a pool hot and unique.

We're wet.

Untamed.

Basking in the beauty of the island and this summer together. Sam pants in my ear, her loud breaths cheering me on and driving me to thrust faster.

Harder.

Deeper.

Leaning my forehead to hers, I take over completely and roll my hips upward while I press her down. "Do I make you feel good, gorgeous?" I ask gruffly.

"God... yes." She covers my mouth with hers, and her chest expands against my hard body, her wet breasts rubbing across my pecs.

It's erotic.

The water reaches my chin, and I drown in her, burying myself as far inside her as possible.

My balls meet the curve of her ass with each thrust.

Adrenaline shoots down my spine.

And my release comes fast and hard, slamming into me with a feral vehemence.

It takes me by surprise, and it seems to do the same with Sam as her high-pitched moan fills the quiet evening.

"Shit," I mutter, digging my fingers into her hair and holding on as my body pulses with blissful satisfaction.

Sam shakes in my arms, and the ripples across the surface of the water grow, diminishing toward the opposite ends.

I didn't see this woman coming, but she burst into my life with her ruffled pink dresses and strappy sandals.

Her matching gym sets and dirty sneakers from so many jump squats and miles ran in them.

Her refreshing sense of humor and big heart.

As I hold her in my arms, it feels like my life is just beginning, and my chest stirs with a feeling I've never known before.

Chapter 13
SAMANTHA

I spin on my tiptoes in the middle of the kitchen, humming and floating on a blissful high from last night.

I take one look at the pool outside and tingle all over.

My morning shoulder workout in the hotel gym was also productive, and I felt stronger than usual, probably due to my carb intake from yesterday. It's why cheat meals are so important to me. Other than being essential for a balanced lifestyle, carbs shock my metabolism and boost my energy.

And it didn't hurt that I had extra energy after the orgasms Xander gave me last night.

While the coffee brews, I check my phone for unread texts and see they're all from Val.

Val: You. Sneaky. Bitch.

Val: You and Xander? XANDER?

Val: Where have you two been hiding?

Val: You never called me! I was upset, but then I saw how busy you've been ;)

Val: But seriously... CALL ME.

Before I have a chance to answer, the phone rings in my hand, and my brother's name flashes across the top.

"Why the fuck am I looking at a picture of you and my best friend on the internet looking like you're on your damn honeymoon with an announcement that *he's* your mystery boyfriend?" Teddy's rushed voice booms out of the speaker.

I set it on the kitchen counter and wipe the sleep from my eyes. It's too early for this decibel, but it doesn't stop me from messing with one of my favorite people. "Because we eloped. I thought that was clear."

"What?" he rages.

I bet his cheeks are puffed out like Dad's get when his top football teams lose. Or when we steal from Dad's secret stash of candy. Recently diagnosed with diabetes, Mom has him on a strict diet, but Teddy and I know he keeps a pile of sweets in the garage that he digs into for his own sanity.

"I'm going to kill that motherfucker. I told him what would happen if he laid a finger on you, and now I'm going to have to cut his—"

"Whoa, whoa." I speak up to ensure he can hear me as I grab my mug of coffee, steam rising out of it as I lean on the opposite counter. "Deep breaths, big brother. I'm just kidding."

"What?" he repeats, but with much less hostility.

"Teddy, the post is a lie. Xander is just helping me get out of a dicey situation." I sigh, immediately glancing toward his bedroom door.

I slept in his bed last night—well, we didn't do much sleeping.

But no one has to know, especially not my brother, until we're ready to tell them.

"Explain," he clips.

"You saw the nasty shit I was taking over the whole mess with the wardrobe malfunction, and then Jason posted a series of videos bashing me, claiming he and I were never together. He even posted pictures with another woman to make people think she's been his girlfriend this whole time and not me."

He scoffs. "Pathetic."

"Even so, it was all so humiliating, but I couldn't let him take away all that I've built. He might've gained a host of new followers because of me, but I couldn't let him win. I needed an announcement that was a lot juicier than anything Jason was spewing."

"The fucking prick," Teddy grinds out.

I reach for a banana from the fruit bowl as I continue. "So, Xander offered to stand in as my boyfriend, and in turn, he's already gained several new followers himself. I suspect my merchandise sales will be back up in no time too. As you might've noticed, neither of our reputations were exactly glowing a week ago, and we turned it around." Silence answers me, and I check to make sure he's still on the line. "Teddy?"

"There's really nothing going on between you two?" he asks, the hesitation in his voice heavy.

His question might as well be sitting on my chest like an anchor.

Biting my lip, I force myself to sound convincing. "No."

Okay, not the most confident response I've ever given, but it's all I can manage. Saying anything more would blow the whole thing wide open, and I wouldn't put it past Teddy to board the next flight out here just to kick Xander's ass.

I'm lying to protect him, really.

Teddy's loud exhale is confusing, and I stare at my phone

until I hear him again. "I'm glad he's taking care of you and that you're having a good time. You deserve the break."

My chest warms.

"You're coming back for Dad's sixtieth birthday party, though, right? He won't appreciate the barbershop quartet without his ray of sunshine." He chuckles, and I picture him rubbing a hand down his face.

"He sure knows how to have fun." I lean my hip against the counter as the door to Xander's room opens slowly. He tiptoes across the sitting room and into the kitchen, careful to stay away from the phone like I'm on FaceTime. I hold it up to show him it's a regular call, although I'm not sure it's necessary.

Teddy knows we're here together, so seeing us both wouldn't raise any flags.

But we can't be too sure, I guess.

"I need to go. Call you later?" I say to Teddy while Xander stalks toward me, his hair mussed and crazed from our late-night escapades.

And he's shirtless. Did I mention how unfair it is that his abs are so lean and carved out more perfectly than if he would've drawn them on? He's never even had to eat kale to look like that.

I do enjoy the view, though.

In fact, my mouth waters as I take a slow bite of my banana, my attention on him as he cracks his knuckles like he's preparing for something... sexy.

After I end the call, Xander scoops me into his arms and hoists me onto the kitchen counter, my half-eaten banana tossed next to us. He plants a greedy kiss to my lips, and I squeeze my legs around his waist.

"I was looking forward to waking up next to you, but you weren't in bed when I opened my eyes," he mumbles, exaggerating a pout, and I nip at his plump bottom lip.

"That's because I went to the gym, then did a few body-weight exercises outside." I kiss him again as he toys with the waistband of my shorts. "There's a good little spot to run steps and do tricep dips. Burpees too, of course."

He moves his palm down to my thigh and slides his fingers up my shorts. "I thought hiking would be our exercise for the day. Besides sex, anyway."

"Both are commendable workouts, which is why I took it easy this morning and didn't use heavy weights." I interlock my fingers behind his neck and latch onto his lips, drinking him in like the ocean absorbs a river.

"You must be worn out," he whispers, taking one hand out of my shorts and reaching for something in my periphery.

I hum against him, enjoying the mint on his tongue this morning—the morning after great pool sex and two more rounds in bed. He was slow and sensual. Fast and mind-blowing.

Horizontally and vertically.

Every way we did it was magic.

"Let me feed my queen," he says in a low voice as a teasing smile plays across his expression.

I pull back, and he's holding my banana up for me. Through my laughter, I make a show of taking a big bite and chewing more loudly than would be socially acceptable if we were in public.

And if I was with anyone but Xander.

When it comes to him, he doesn't care how messy I am. How much sand is caked in my hair. If I'm wearing makeup or not.

He wants *me*.

He sees beyond the filters and coy captions. The sponsored posts and scripted live videos. Being with Xander has been an experience, even better than snuba diving with sea turtles in paradise.

And I want to soak in the sunshine a little while longer.

"What did your brother say?" he asks, stepping out from between my legs to grab a mug out of the cabinet.

"He saw the post." I hop down from the counter. "So, I told him we eloped."

He whirls around, more wide-eyed than the baby pig who barreled into his old room. "You did what?" He leans on the sink like his legs turned to jelly.

Rolling my eyes, I take the mug from him for fear he'll drop and break it. "Relax," I say over my shoulder and pop a K-cup into the Keurig. "I just explained the situation and that you're helping me out. Which isn't a lie."

"He was still pissed, wasn't he?" He curses under his breath and shakes his head. "We should've told him the plan before you posted, but now he's blindsided. He's going to use my body as a punching bag until I'm hanging there dead," he rambles as the coffee drips into his mug.

He continues mumbling about all the ways he's betrayed Teddy as I finish off my banana, no break in his rant to let me jump in until he finally stops to take a deep inhale.

"Are you done?" I quirk an eyebrow and set a steaming cup in front of him, then bring mine up to my lips to blow on it. "He was actually appreciative."

"That's what he said?" he asks with the gravity of confirming a volcanic eruption.

Why is he so freaked out? He knew the risks involved. He's the one who told me to post our "relationship" last night.

I know we lied to my brother—and the world. It sucks, but technically, it's *not* a lie, since we did sleep together several times. If anything, he should be confused over the web of half-truths and ruses we've weaved like I am, but instead, he's terrified.

"What's going on?" I ask, studying him.

"Nothing." He shrugs. "I'm just... surprised by his calm response, is all."

"Right," I draw out.

"I mean it." His shoulders slump, and after a pause, his grim frown finally transforms into a grin as he reaches out to caress my forearm. "I'm also wondering what shirt to wear on our hike. Should I go with the whale tank that looks like it was meant for a toddler, or do I wear the shark shirt that has a fin sticking out of the back?"

Giggling, I nearly spill my hot drink. "It does *not* have a fin."

"It doesn't, but wouldn't that be cool as fuck?" Amusement fills his expression, further replacing the fear from before, and it eases my nerves.

Besides, my brother's reaction was—and is—something I'm scared of too, but we don't have to worry about that any time soon.

Xander and I have a list to get through first.

"Go with the whale tank," I say.

He claps and walks backward toward his room, his coffee forgotten on the counter. "I'll do my best not to outshine you."

When he disappears to change, I go into my own room to do the same, but first, I check my phone. I have hundreds of notifications, including some from friends in the industry. The newest message is from Kendall, a fellow influencer and friend from LA, expressing how cute Xander and I are together and that she's happy for me. In the message above it, she says if I need anything to let her know.

She's so kind. Her giving heart is what drew me to her in the first place. At the time, she was just starting her fitness journey, and I could tell after one workout that she had a lot of grit and light to share with the world.

After I respond to thank her for reaching out, I check some of the other notifications. There's nothing new from Jason, thankfully, but many of the comments ask for the story of how Xander and I met.

Where he took me on our first date.

What my brother thinks.

They're all questions I'll need to figure out how to answer... eventually.

I'm about to click my phone off when it vibrates with an incoming call.

"You and Xander?" Val screeches the second I swipe to answer.

Clutching the phone to my ear, I ensure the door is closed and say, "It's not what you think."

"*Please* tell me what it is," she begs. "And it better be good news because I've had a week from hell. Not that you would know since you haven't called."

"I'm sorry, okay?" I grab a shirt and pace by the bed.

"It's fine. I already forgave you."

"Then why are you giving me shit?"

"Because I wouldn't be myself if I didn't. Duh," she tosses back, and I imagine her dipping her chin onto one shoulder in a not-so-innocent manner that makes me smile.

"Are you okay?"

"We're talking about you now," she insists. "Spill."

I tell my friend the truth. The one I told Teddy, anyway. I only get halfway through it before Val interrupts me. "How many times have you slept with him?"

"What?" I ask nervously and glance toward the door again like Xander might hear us.

"I can't even see your face, and I still know you're lying. You've totally slept with him!"

Sighing, I relent. How can I lie to my best friend? "Fine. You caught me."

Her response is a whisper-scream of excitement that makes me squeeze my eyes closed.

"Four times," I say with amused victory in my voice. I'm ecstatic , really, as I finally let the truth free.

Especially since Val is as excited as I am.

"That is what I'm fucking talking about, S." There's a thud on her end like she dropped something, possibly her fist on a table, which makes me wonder where she is for such a private conversation.

"I'll give you all the details when I get back," I offer. "Now, why has your week sucked?"

She groans. "Poetry Simon and I broke up on the way back from our trip."

"Are you serious? Isn't this the third time you've ended things?"

"Don't remind me," she warns. "Anyway, those details also need to be delivered in person over a bottle of a Napa Valley red."

"It's a date."

Once we promise to talk soon, we end the call, but I don't toss my phone aside.

Instead, I click to add a photo of Xander and me at the beach to my profile. In the picture, he has sand smeared on his cheek in the shape of a cloud. His smile is uniquely Xander—fun, carefree, and unapologetic.

He's also watching me with a curiosity I can't explain or describe, but I know how it makes me feel.

Giddy and important.

For the caption, I type out *From #GymBae to #BeachBae* and press to share it, enjoying the side-by-side pictures of Xander and me wrapped in each other's arms on my page.

I like it a lot.

"Y ou're right—that whale shirt was made for a toddler and got put in the wrong section." I snort and tug at the hem of his bright purple T-shirt, which fits snugly around his biceps. "We could go shopping at an actual store, you know."

"But then I wouldn't have these awesome conversation starters."

I skip to keep up with his strides along the dirt trail. My legs are long, but I have a slower pace than him, especially since I'm on the lookout for good photo ops. This is definitely the place to stock up on good content. I'll need more of Xander and me too— in order to keep up pretenses and not because I like pictures of us piling up in my album, of course.

The one I got of his back while he walked ahead was a good shot. Banyan trees stood tall on either side of the path, and he looked like an ant, comparatively.

I want more of those candid shots, where we're lost in nature, especially now that we're out in the open. Xander looks larger than life out here, a relaxed air about him that's contagious.

"That's never been an issue between us," I say.

"No, but it was helpful when Gladys stopped me at the café the other day."

"Mr. Logan, do I need to be jealous of this woman?" I nudge him with my shoulder.

He chuckles. "No, no. Her husband, Edgar, made it very clear that I was too young for her."

"So, you two parted amicably?"

"Right after I paid for her coffee because Edgar ran off with her wallet when he thought he saw a Kiwikiu outside. I did add them to my character notebook, though. She was quirky, especially when she described the owl she saw in a Koa tree like it was a talking animal. I should include her in a show or movie someday."

"I have a lot of questions." I grin, watching where I step for any holes or branches.

"I have one of my own." He spins and walks sideways to face me, a gleam in his eye that's sparkling with a dangerous mix of curiosity and mischief. *What is he up to?* "What does jealousy look like on Samantha Ray?"

My exhale comes out with a whoosh and turns into a giggle. I thought his question would be more devious than that. "I don't get jealous," I simply state.

As he falls back into step next to me, his laugh echoes around us, making it feel like we're the only two people on earth. We haven't run into a single person yet, and it's been peaceful.

"Okay, I confess." I eye him as we continue ahead. "There was this one time..."

He rubs his hands together. "Go on."

"His name was Tony Garfield, and I was jealous when he shared his animal crackers with Megan Jones instead of me." I nod, my cheeks red from trying to keep a straight face. "It made elementary school pretty tough."

"Where'd you go afterward?"

"What do you mean?"

"Obviously, you had to have transferred schools after the heartbreak you experienced," he jokes.

"I thought we already established that I don't cry over jerks." I lean into him and walk along the curve in the path, which quickly becomes less recognizable as such. Instead, footsteps of other hikers in the mud lead us in the right direction.

That, and the map we got from the hotel helps guide us through the jungle of banyan trees, which later spits us out onto a clearer trail along the edge of a drop-off.

Eventually, we come to an overlook, and my feet stop, along with my heart.

"Wow," I breathe.

Green mountainside stretches tall and strong across the island, and the winds are gustier at this elevation. The loose strands of my hair fly backward and out of my eyes as if the wind didn't want me to miss this view. It feels like we're untouchable up here, and we haven't even reached the highest point yet.

It's times like these when I feel connected to something bigger than myself. Something significant and meaningful. A rare and inspiring experience.

This trip has been full of those, and when Xander sneaks his hand into mine, I'm overwhelmed with gratitude.

I grip it tightly like I'll fall off the edge otherwise, and it grounds me more firmly than if I were to carve out my name on one of the trees ahead.

As we continue down the path hand in hand, he breaks the silence and asks, "Why Samantha Ray? You could've picked anything for your brand name."

"Um..." I gulp as nostalgia overcomes me, the knot of emotion from this hike rendering me nearly speechless. "My mom had a miscarriage after she had Teddy. She and my dad didn't think they'd be able to have any more children, but then I came along three years later. Ever since I can remember, they've called me their miracle. Their ray of sunshine. I didn't even think twice about the name."

"I had no idea." He comes to a complete stop and peers over at me, intensity setting his eyes ablaze. "I love it."

I squeeze his hand tighter as we sway along the path, our pace slower than when we first started in order to take in more of the scenery.

When we come to a waterfall, my jaw drops again.

This island has amazed me beyond words on numerous occasions, this moment included.

The small clearing is lined with lush and healthy ferns, as well as other greenery, and the splash of the waterfall is even and powerful.

Breathtaking.

I inhale a deep breath like I'm absorbing the inspiration for my soul.

In a way, I am.

There's nothing more fulfilling than adventure and natural beauty, but experiencing it with Xander elevates this to a whole new level.

Because I care about him, and it's special to be on this life-changing trip together.

"Come on." He leads me around the edge of the pool toward the waterfall, underneath which a few women pose for selfies.

While we wait our turn, we strip down to our swimsuits to get ready to wade into the water.

"It's going to be hard when we go back, and I have to wear regular clothes. At this point, my bikini is my second skin," I joke as I follow him into the shallow part.

He stops when the water reaches his hip and pulls me toward him, the edge of the ripples an inch way. "Island living looks good on you." He pecks me on the mouth, and I suspect it's a quick and chaste one because we're not completely alone, even though it might've felt like it during most of the hike.

And this is how we spend the rest of our trek. Laughing, stealing kisses behind—and against—trees, and holding hands. We talk about his mom's current projects—one of which has her filming in Paris for the next few weeks—and about his TV show coming up too.

Although I'm happy to get my fill of his life, it also reminds me of the reality waiting for us back in LA.

I've started to feel more like myself this week, especially since I took a break from social media. Even though it wasn't planned, it was exactly what I needed to recharge. It's given me perspective and urged me to live in the moment.

The encouragement from so many of my friends and followers has also been a huge relief, and it helps to know they're in my corner. That they'll be there when I get online in a full capacity again.

But I'm not ready to go home.

I want to stretch out this fantasy for as long as possible before we get back to the grind—and before Xander and I have to face our situation head-on.

It's inevitable. He's not some guy I met here on vacation and will never see again. He's my brother's best friend—Xander is *my* friend. He's part of my life, and I want to keep it that way.

We might've crossed those platonic boundaries, but at our core, we have a connection beyond lust.

At least, I think we do.

I definitely hope it's the same for him, anyway, because what I'm feeling is very real. The butterflies in my stomach are not figments of my imagination or conjured hallucinations from the island.

They're fluttering for Xander.

The guy I let the world believe is my boyfriend.

And even though I was hesitant about the idea at first, it's sounding pretty damn amazing to me now.

Chapter 14
XANDER

"Those pictures don't look fake to me," Teddy chides, a thick warning lying in wait between his words like a shark after its prey.

He's going to lose his shit if he ever finds out about the things I've done to his little sister, and it'll be even worse now that we're lying to him about this fake relationship plan.

"Here's the thing—"

"I know. It's my overprotective brother brain." His sigh comes through the speaker loudly. "I do appreciate you doing her a solid. You're a good friend."

Guilt gnaws at my chest as I stare at my sullen reflection in the bathroom mirror. My shirt is unbuttoned down the front and past my boxers, and my pants are still hanging in the closet. I'm a mess in more ways than one.

"You have your tickets to fly back, right? I haven't heard from Sam, but I told her that Dad is expecting her at his party. You too, I guess." He says the last part with much less enthusiasm.

"Thanks," I deadpan, rubbing a hand down my face. "We

haven't gotten any tickets yet. We've been busy—" I clamp my mouth shut so fast that I almost bite my tongue.

I was so close to letting it slip that Sam and I have been busier exploring each other's bodies than any of the scenery the last few days.

Fuck.

I'm so used to telling Teddy everything, even the embarrassing shit that happens to me, including the time an A-list actress mistook me for her new assistant. Instead of correcting her, I went along with it because she was unfathomably famous, and I thought it would be good to make connections.

Except all I came out of there with was food poisoning from the sushi she'd ordered me as a reward. She just left out the part that it'd been sitting in her car since the night before.

I never thought I'd say this, but I'd rather be back to puking my guts out than having to tell Teddy the truth.

"I'll buy the tickets to leave tomorrow," I blurt, and my face quickly reddens. Did I seriously just tell him we'd leave in less than a fucking day?

"Perfect! See you then, dude."

He clicks off before I can even check in with him and see how he's doing with the fallout of the cougars.

But I can't deny that I'm relieved to have thwarted his suspicions for the time being. I wouldn't offer to leave right away if there was anything going on, right? So, there. Teddy and I are fine.

Except there *is* something going on between his sister and me, and now I have to tell her that I'm cutting our trip short.

Which means we have to get on the same page regarding *us*.

And that also means we'll have to talk sooner rather than later, and I already dread it. I'm not good at this—at telling women how I feel, unless I'm breaking up with them.

It's telling them how much I like and care about them that's the hard part. Harder than picking the first line in a damn script.

Because I do like Sam—more than like her, if I'm honest with myself—but how do I tell her?

There's so much at stake if this relationship flies back to LA with us.

Heart racing, I fish my pants out of the closet, tuck my shirt into the waistband, and smooth my hair back, the strands overdue for a trim. Then I spray cologne on one side of my neck and slide my watch onto my wrist, covering the tattoo there.

I went shopping at an actual mall today while Sam worked out at the gym. I wanted to look presentable next to her at the food and wine festival tonight.

This is the nicest I've looked since we got here.

And something tells me I'm not prepared for what Sam is about to walk out in.

In the living room, I pace in front of the couch, watching my phone, guilt eating at me over what I've done. After a short pause, it vibrates with a new email confirmation that our flight is booked to return home.

No sound has come from Sam's room other than a blow dryer, and I have no idea how long I've been stewing in silence.

Taking a seat, I pull up Instagram and click on her profile to see if anything's changed—and it has.

She's posted an image to her stories of the breakfast cinnamon roll we shared from a local gem, along with our seafood lunch, and there's a new picture of us on her profile from our hike the other day. It makes me smile, but it's definitely not because I'm in it.

It's because of her.

In the image, Sam's hair is damp and wavy over her golden shoulders, and there's a white flower sticking out from behind one ear. I'm looking at her and smiling too, but I don't own the camera like she does—no one compares.

I stare at the picture until I get a new text from Sam, saying she's on the phone with her mom and that I should go ahead to the festival.

Me: Are you not coming?

After a pause, I get a new one from her.

Sam: Sorry. Mom distracted me. Meant to say I'll meet you there when I'm finished!

She follows it up with a kissing emoji, and immediately, my dick stirs. It's a cartoon, but just imagining kissing Sam again makes me hard.

Needy.

We've fucked on every piece of furniture and the floor over the last couple of days, and still, I can't get enough of her.

It's like I'm a teenager again.

As I make my way toward the festival, images of our shower earlier fill my mind, and the taste of her lingers on my tongue.

I need a fucking drink.

The festival is lively, and the sunset is a better backdrop than if it were Photoshopped. Large bouquets of hibiscus line the area around the pool, and I'm wearing a new lei around my neck—a red one today.

I ran into Gladys and Edgar, and they told me all about their hike to find different birds. It gave me more material to add to my notebook, but mostly, it made me smile to see them enjoying the island with each other. Doing something they love.

Like Sam and me.

We've been mistaken for a couple for much of the trip, and our profiles online state as much. It's what we've been acting like too.

And it's been fucking bliss, but I'm on edge. More tense than my shins get when I go running. I even side-eye a server whose tray was empty of seafood appetizers, but I didn't mean it. I just didn't see him.

All I can think about is Sam.

And how much I want to try one of the appetizers.

I find the server again and apologize, then sample three different wines, which is about the time Sam shows up—and it's definitely a show.

I think all heads turn to watch her descend the steps on the other side of the pool, but I can't be certain because my eyes are glued to her.

Between the pots overflowing with brightly colored flowers and greenery, one long leg steps down at a time. At the end of each is a strappy heel that gives her another three inches in height.

Her pale green dress hugs her body in a sinful way, but what's sexier is the slit that runs up to her midthigh.

I drag my gaze up over her perky breasts and take in her wavy hair, one side tucked behind her ear and held there by a white flower much like the one from the picture earlier.

And she smiles at me.

How she spots me in this crowd of people, I have no idea. But she walks around the edge of the pool toward me, twinkling lights strung above her and around the perimeter. It gives her an even brighter glow than the natural one she wears.

I set my wineglass on a table. Or at least I think I do. I could've tossed it into the pool for all I know.

The only thing I'm aware of is that my feet are moving to meet Sam halfway past a few white tents, where people's chatter and the music are all muffled. If this were a TV show or movie, the musical score would start slow and soft, then quicken and crescendo up to the moment I reach her.

I wrap my arms around her, dip her head back, and cover her mouth with mine.

But it's not just any kiss. It's a connection I feel in my damn soul—something I've never felt before. I've never experienced even a fraction of it.

"You are absolutely fucking beautiful," I whisper, bringing her to stand upright.

She sways against me, and I keep my arms wrapped around her waist, breathing in her coconut scent. "You don't look half-bad yourself." She smooths her palms down my pale blue dress shirt. "I thought the hotel gift shop only had toddler clothes."

"I couldn't show up here in a whale shirt, and the only other halfway decent button-up I found, I wore to dinner the other night and got cocktail sauce on." I chuckle. "So, I went to the mall."

"You went without me? When?" She twirls the hair at the nape of my neck between her fingers, causing a new wave of tension to roll down my spine, especially with her swollen lips so close.

They're pouty and adorable, and she's making me see fucking stars.

"While you were at the gym." I pull back, but not before I grab her hand and lead her toward one of the tents for a glass of wine. "There's a lot you can do instead of working out, you know. The time you'd be given…"

"*Some* of us have to work at our bodies and can't just roll out of bed with a six-pack," she throws at me.

I come to a stop at the tent with the best wine I've tried so far, grab a couple of glasses, and wait our turn, as the crowd seems to have tripled in size in the last five minutes. "Okay, you've worn me down. I'll tell you my secret."

"Please do." Her eyes light up, amusement and curiosity etched in her smile.

I lean in close until her hair tickles my nose. "Sex."

Her tiny gasp is full of shock.

"We've burned so many calories this week, and I think we're well on our way to competing in bodybuilding." I chuckle and place a lingering kiss to her temple.

"We could even win." She peers up at me and bites her lip.

"You want to kiss me again, don't you?" I quirk my eyebrow in challenge... and hope.

Instead of answering out loud, she cups my cheek and kisses me.

I'd do this all night if we were alone, but the line of eager winos nudges us toward the front for our pours.

Full glasses in hand, we work our way through the crowd back toward the pool, where water shoots from the edges in a curved manner to the other side in rainbow fashion.

"What should we toast to?" I ask, holding my drink up.

"To burning more calories," she says, narrowing her gaze.

"I've never enjoyed fitness more."

We clink and sip and steal wine-soaked kisses while we stroll through the festival. The sun has completely set by the time we come across two familiar faces—the Italian couple from the beach.

Francesca's jaw drops. "You're here!" She taps her husband's shoulder, then points. "Look who it is."

"Hi," Sam says as she gives Francesca a hug. When she

pulls back, she slides her hand into mine again like it's second nature, and I squeeze it back.

Francesca starts to say something but stops when she sees our interlocked fingers. "You two make a beautiful couple—I just knew there was something between you, even though you denied it."

"Oh... we... well..." Sam and I talk over each other, sputtering like we've forgotten how to speak in full sentences.

"We're enjoying the island and having fun," I offer hesitantly, suddenly nervous.

My panic climbs a notch when Sam withdraws her hand from mine, and the reality of what I've done is slowly starting to peek through the curtains I drew over my brain when Sam showed up.

I need to talk to her.

"Of course," Mario says, stepping closer. "Don't mind my wife. She has love on the brain."

"As she should," Sam coos. "You two are on your honeymoon. It's all about the romance."

The pair embraces, and Francesca looks up at him with moony eyes that most would consider sweet.

I've never had a woman look at me like that before, her affection and care obvious and genuine. Lust? I've had plenty of that. Many women I've been with have wanted sex from me. A good time. Some laughs.

Or they wanted me to introduce them to my mother, a producer, or anyone else who could launch their career in Hollywood.

I've never had anything real, and the fact that I kept getting burned might've been why I stopped searching for it.

"Will you come back tomorrow?" Francesca asks. "An Italian winemaker will be sharing a few stories and secrets of his experience in Tuscany. It's going to be amazing."

"That sounds great." Sam turns to me. "We don't have any set plans for tomorrow night, so we could—"

"Actually, we're leaving in the morning," I blurt.

"What? No," Francesca draws out with a frown.

"What do you mean?" Sam asks, angling her body now to fully face me.

"Will you excuse us, please?" I take Sam by the elbow and lead her away, my stomach knotted and nerves rattled.

"What's going on?" she asks from behind me.

I continue leading her away from the noise and around to the front of the resort until we get somewhere quieter.

"Xander," she calls out and pulls her arm from my grasp. My name leaves her lips with annoyance and confusion, and I grind my teeth together in order to maintain control. "You bought us tickets to leave tomorrow? When were you planning on telling me?"

"Tonight."

Her expression falls as she wraps her arms around her midsection.

I sigh. "We were going to have to leave at some point, Sam. We can't stay here forever."

"I know that." She purses her lips and pins me with a glare. "I'm just blindsided that you didn't talk to me first. I mean, tomorrow is... It's so soon..."

I avert my gaze as piano music from the lobby filters through the opening doors, and a few people emerge. They're happy, and I just wish I had something to throw at them.

Scratching my head, I say, "I'm sorry, but Teddy called earlier and insisted we come back. He was already suspicious of our relationship announcement online, and I didn't want to give him any more reason to think something's going on between us. I panicked and promised him we'd leave tomorrow."

"But there is something going on."

"Yes, but—"

"Hey! Aren't you Samantha Ray?" A woman who looks younger than both of us appears at our side, her smile wide like she struck gold. I swear if I looked hard enough, I'd see stars in her eyes. "Oh my God, is this your *gym bae* Xander?"

Sam clears her throat and snakes her arm through mine, a mask falling over her entire demeanor like I've seen actors do when they slip into character. "It is."

The woman squeals every other syllable while she tells us her name is Scarlett, and she's here with her father, a sommelier from LA.

"Can I please take a selfie with you two?" Scarlett asks. "It would make this trip with my dad *so* worth it, especially since he's spent the whole time talking about wine, cheese, and wine and cheese pairings."

"Of course." Sam leans in for the camera, with a smile that doesn't even seem forced.

I blink, trying to shake off the whiplash of how we were on the verge of an argument, but she's now laughing with a stranger as smoothly as if she were giving the girl fitness tips.

"Get in here!" Scarlett waves for me.

"Sure," I say, and it's the only word I've contributed to this entire interaction.

In the camera, I look like I just wrestled a boar and lost. My hair is tousled from the wind, and my eyes are frowning, not to mention my shirt is untucked on one side from tugging at it in frustration.

Pretend.

I need to pretend.

I plaster on a smile, and Scarlett snaps about fifty photos, at the very least. By the end of the encounter, she calls us her best friends and rushes off to send them all to her "frenemy," who's going to regret not taking her to Coachella last year.

Evidently, they've both been following Sam for a couple years now and have completed all her workout guides. They've lived by her nutrition plan too. Scarlett gushed about the kiwi dessert, in particular, which she said she makes every week.

It made Sam blush, and although I'm happy she has a ton of people who look up to her like that, I'm beyond confused.

"Is it so terrible if we tell my brother about us?" Sam resumes like there was no interruption at all.

She was laughing with Scarlett, and now she's scowling at me.

But at the mention of her brother, my chest expands with guilt, and my fucking heart drowns in it. "What would we even say?"

"That we like each other." She lets out a sound that resembles something between a laugh and scoff. "We'd tell him the truth."

"You don't even know how to tell a bunch of strangers the truth, let alone Teddy." I wave my hand in the direction Scarlett just disappeared. "Exhibit fucking A."

She stands back with her lips parted and hurt in her eyes.

"Come on, Sam," I plead. "You hide so much of yourself online. All your pictures and videos are pristine—every hair in place, no sweat to be seen. It's like you're embarrassed you work so hard." I lick my lips, my throat clogging up with each truth pressed against the walls of it, begging to be let out. "You were too scared to tell your followers that Jason was your mystery boyfriend, but he dumped you. You were so terrified of being honest that you had to pretend to date me. And it worked too. The pictures of us are selling the lie, and you love it."

"That was your idea." She jabs her finger into my chest, but I barely feel it with the turmoil numbing it. "If you were so against it, why did you even suggest it?"

"Because I wanted to help you," I whisper. "You were so upset, and all I wanted to do was fix it."

"You did a damn fine job." Her shoulders slump. "Thank you for your service."

The heavy sarcasm in her voice lingers above us like a dark cloud as she brushes past me, but I grip her arm and turn her to face me again. "Sam..."

She dips her head, and when she lifts it back up to meet my gaze, I find tears in her eyes. "I'd take the pictures any day, Xander. The real thing always disappoints."

My chest squeezes as she slips out of my hold.

"You know what's funny about this whole fucking thing?" she snaps. "You're lying too. To yourself and to me. It's not Teddy you're afraid of."

I step back and put distance between us, but it doesn't matter. I already know what she says next is going to sting like a motherfucker.

"What we have—or at least *had*—wasn't just island fun, as you implied. It was real, and it scares you because you've never been in a relationship. You'd rather jump into bed with woman after woman because it's easy. No complications with nuisances like *feelings*," she grinds out. "Trying to say Teddy and your friendship with him has any role in this is just a bullshit excuse to cover up the fact that you're a damn coward. I lied on my profile because it benefitted my business, but I would never run away from a chance at something true just because it was messy or difficult."

She turns her back to me and walks away without waiting for a response. Not that I have one to give.

Sadly—and admittedly, cowardly—it even relieves me not to, because it would be too hard to profess out loud that everything she said about me is true.

I am afraid.

I don't want to look her brother—my best friend—in the eye and tell him I slept with his sister.

That I have feelings for her but don't know how to be the man she deserves.

Or that it's easier to walk away, no matter how much it pains me.

After one more refill of my wineglass, I slink back up to the room—the room we share for one last night—and find the main area empty, except for the heels she was wearing tonight. Each one is tossed to the opposite side of the room like she jerked them off in a hurried rage before disappearing into her bedroom.

We should've been throwing our clothes to the side with passion, not anger.

And it just makes me feel shittier.

I grab a beer from the fridge and trudge to my room, my feet heavy.

The things I said and did were shitty, but part of me still believes Sam has been putting up a facade, online and with me. How am I supposed to know where Samantha Ray ends and Sam West begins?

It's hard for someone in her position and career to know where the line is between an online presence and the true self— I just witnessed it firsthand.

She was vulnerable and lost when we got to the island, and I was there for her. I'm the only guy she knows within thousands of miles. How does she know she *really* wants me?

As I lay my head back onto a pillow, my clothes untouched, I ask myself that question repeatedly.

Beyond my fear of starting an actual relationship with her, I'm scared to find out I've fallen for someone who doesn't genuinely feel the same way about me.

I toss and turn all night with these nagging insecurities until

I finally jolt awake, but when I go into the living room, I wish I was still asleep.

Sam's heels are gone from the sitting room.

There's no coffee brewing, blow dryer blasting from her bathroom, or music echoing from the balcony.

There's only a note waiting for me on the counter. Scrolled across the top of a notepad with the hotel letterhead is a message from Sam that she got her own flight and left this morning.

As if that wasn't bad enough, she further twisted the knife in my gut by writing that she sent me money via Venmo for the roundtrip ticket because she doesn't want to owe me anything.

I curse under my breath and crumple the piece of paper in my fist, then march into my room to get dressed.

Reality is waiting for me.

Chapter 15
SAMANTHA

That fucking asshole.

I groan in the bathroom of my parents' home as cheerful music floats through the locked door. I'm not in the mood for a party. I'm more in the salty, give-me-a-knife emotional place because I could easily use it to tear up everything Jason loves the most in this world—his sneakers.

"S? Are you in there?" Val's voice rises over the music as she taps on the door. "If it's you, let me in. If it's not, let me in, anyway, because I have to pee."

I throw the door open and pull her inside.

"Oh, thank God it's you." She whirls around to face me. "For a second, I feared it was your uncle Hubert, who's made quite a few passes at me tonight."

"You *are* single now," I say weakly as I check my reflection, fluffing my wavy hair over both shoulders.

"Don't even joke about me being that desperate." She nudges me with her shoulder, and I sway sideways as she leans on the counter. "What are you in here stewing over?"

"I'm not stewing." I cross both arms over my chest, my silk

dress soft and smooth against my skin. "I'm plotting a murder of some prized sneakers."

"Let me take my earrings out first," she plays along, her laugh soft and comforting, but I know she would also chuck her shoes and kick some ass if I needed it.

She's had my back since college, and her support has been a constant in my life.

We shared much more than a dorm and each other's clothes. Val and I both aspired to work for ourselves someday. We didn't know what our dreams would become or that we'd achieve more than we thought possible. In fact, we believed we were asking a lot in the bulleted entrepreneurial bucket list we crafted over virgin daiquiris during our freshman year.

But that list grew wings and flew.

Unlike my other friends, Val knows all too well what it's like to run an unconventional business. She doesn't get offended or angry when I have to miss drinks at a new club or sushi night in Malibu. Rather, Val understands the constant hustle required to be successful, and she never holds it against me, and vice versa. I get that her work requires odd hours too, and it's how we've both gotten to where we are.

Although we're in different industries, the dedication and sacrifices are similar, and I'll always be grateful that we rose through the ranks together.

I'm lucky to have her here tonight too.

I unlock my phone and click play on the video—Jason's latest and sleaziest move in this game I never agreed to play.

Jason's voice quickly fills the bathroom, and he tells the world I've been lying about Xander. That Jason himself was my mystery guy, and he has hundreds of pictures to prove it. He ends the video with a laugh as he tells his viewers how manipulative and pathetic I am for stringing my followers along.

The worst part about it is that he's right. I could do without his malicious tone and mockery, but Jason fucking *Douche* is right.

Xander was right about me too.

And the comments are spot-on, which make me want to throw up even more.

I care too much about my image to be and live what I preach —being totally honest and true about my successes, as well as my pitfalls. And this is my punishment for losing sight of my core values.

My other sentence is losing Xander.

It's been four days since we returned from our trip. Well, I assume he's back in LA, anyway. I haven't seen or spoken to him since the night of the wine and food festival. Since he gave voice to all my insecurities, then retreated like the scared little boy I realized he is.

We all have our flaws, but he used mine against me and ran away.

Each day that's passed, I've alternated from pissed to hurt to sad, and then back from the beginning again in a painful cycle.

I thought our trip would be an innocent and fun escape, but it threw my world into more chaos than it was when I left it.

"I'm definitely taking my earrings out and heading straight to Jason's." Val hands the phone back to me. "I'll call you when I've buried the body."

For the first time tonight, I giggle. My best friend has that effect on me.

"I'm so glad you're here, even though it's not exactly a wild night, and my uncle is harassing you—I'll talk to him, by the way," I assure her.

"Please do, because I'd hate to use an uppercut to that weak jaw of his like we learned in self-defense class." She sighs and rubs my upper arms. "I feel that now is as good a time as ever to tell you..."

I narrow my gaze. "Tell me what?"

"Xander got here right before I knocked on the door." She grimaces, tucking her arms away and behind her back. "That's what I came in here to tell you."

"Oh." I nod, and my heart squeezes as tightly as the oranges in my juicer.

"If you want to sneak out of here early, I can create a diversion, like kiss Hubert on the cheek. I think it would stop his heart long enough to let you escape, but not so long that it kills him, of course."

Again, I giggle, even though my stomach is a mess. I don't even get this nauseous after eating a bacon cheeseburger with extra cheese, which I rarely have anymore.

"I can have a bottle of vodka at your house faster than you can say *Val is a genius*." She winks.

"I'll be fine," I tell her and squeeze her hands in mine, then drop them and pace the small bathroom. "You know what frustrates me the most?"

"I imagine—"

"That Xander caught me so off guard that night on Maui." Anger rolls over my chest in waves, and I scoff. "There were so many things I should've said to him—like the fact that he's a dick and doesn't get me at all like I thought he did—but I couldn't fucking think straight."

At some point during my flustered rambling, Val took a seat on the edge of the bathtub, from where she stares up at me. "Would it make you feel better if you told him?"

I slump against the counter, and with one flash of understanding across her expression, it's obvious I don't need to give her any other answer. During moments like this, it's also very clear that she's good at what she does for a living as an advice columnist.

"I was serious about sneaking out early." She rises, smoothing her palms over a high-waisted faux leather miniskirt.

I make a mental note to borrow it when I'm feeling better and ready to be part of the world again. I just have a huge mess to deal with first.

"Thank you." I expect her to follow, but Val inches toward the toilet in the corner, instead. "You coming?"

"I was actually serious about needing to pee too." She shifts from one foot to the other in the familiar dance of a full bladder. "I'll only be a minute, and I'll come find you."

As I rejoin the party, the barbershop quartet makes its way around the living room, serenading my parents and their friends, who sway and smile like they're transported by the music.

It makes me happy to see them celebrating like this, and it's even better that we're reptile free for the evening since they checked Rico, Rattle, and Reggie into a boarding facility for the night. They said they take them once a month as a minivacation for them, and Teddy and I managed to hold in our laughs until we were alone in the kitchen.

Our parents' quirks never cease to amaze us.

I come to a stop by my mom and feel a heated gaze travel over me. Sudden adrenaline courses through my body, and I don't have to look up to know Xander's tracing every inch of me with his heated stare.

When I turn around, I get more than I anticipate. He's deeply tanned from our vacation, and it only reminds me of how much fun we had.

How much I miss him.

But I'm mad at him too.

So many emotions slam into me.

Yesterday morning, I forgot that I'd scheduled a picture of

us to post on my Instagram, and when I saw it on my profile, I stopped and zoomed in.

It was breathtaking, and I didn't just think that because of the waterfall in the background. It was Xander's shining eyes that captivated me.

Then the anger set back in, and I posted five times since then just to bury the photo on my page. I never post that many times in a single day, but it was worth the break in my consistency in order to have something other than Xander's stupid perfect grin right at the top of my profile.

No matter the motive, it was a good excuse to start posting more fitness and nutrition content again too, which is the main focus of my platform, anyway.

With Jason's new video, I'll have to respond or decide if I want to block him and carry on with rebuilding my business without his stink all over it.

The latter might be the way to go. Otherwise, this shit will never blow over.

When the small crowd gathered in the living room claps, I snap out of my trance and swallow to wet my dry throat as I make my way to the dining table. Tall bottles are lined up in a neat row as a makeshift bar, and I pour myself a drink.

I take a sip and turn to find Xander approaching me.

Teddy is nowhere in sight, and neither is Val.

We're alone.

"I'm surprised you came tonight." I study him over the rim of my cup, my heart rate three times faster than it was a moment ago.

"I told Teddy days ago that I'd be here, so I'm here." He fixes a drink for himself, his arm brushing my hip where it rests against the edge of the table.

I practically jump at the contact. "Right. And Teddy is so

important to you that you didn't care who else might be here who might not want to see you."

"If that was true, you wouldn't have posted a picture of you and me yesterday," he shoots back and takes a long sip of whatever dark drink he just made.

I was too distracted by the way his arm muscles tightened and loosened while he moved to notice what alcohol he used.

My eyes snap to his. "I forgot that I scheduled it before we left the island," I explain, a sharp edge in each word. "By the time I saw it, it already had ten thousand likes and several hundred comments. If I would've deleted it at that point, I would've looked like a jackass."

"And it's all about appearances," he says sarcastically, and I'm rattled. The man infuriates me worse than anything Jason ever did. "This may be none of *my* business, but how long are you planning on using me for your publicity stunt?" he asks, his sarcasm even deeper than before.

There are a million comebacks on the tip of my tongue—including the fact that it was *his* freaking idea in the first place—but the truth is, none of it would solve our problem.

We told my nearly two million followers that he and I are together, and I never thought about what would happen if we drifted apart. I didn't think we ever would. Then again, I hadn't expected anything that happened over the last few weeks.

When we were wrapped in each other's arms, exploring every sensual spot on both our bodies, it was like we had all the time in the world. Nothing could reach us on that island, and we were too solid to break apart.

I was wrong on so many levels.

"I'm done playing games, Sam," Xander whispers as he brushes past me.

But I stop him, grasping his forearm and tugging him backward. "For the record, I didn't force you to help me. You're the one who offered. You're the one who gave me the push to post the announcement. So stop acting like I'm the bad guy here who manhandled you into this agreement."

He clenches his jaw and grinds out, "I didn't realize it was a lifelong contract. Nor did you mention it would bring out this... disappointing side of you." His voice grows softer, and guilt swims in his dark brown eyes like he surprised even himself with that admission.

I gulp, but it doesn't go down easily. The lump in my throat only grows the longer I stand here in front of him. We're planted a foot from each other, and I'm still holding his arm, a connection between us.

But we might as well be miles apart.

"I know I have my flaws, Xander, but don't blame me for yours."

He doesn't budge as I step closer to him.

"You're disappointed in yourself more than you are me, but it doesn't matter, does it? I wasn't who you thought I was, and you weren't who I thought or needed, either. Let's call it what it is and go our separate ways." I finally drop my hand from him as the pressure builds behind my eyes. The barbershop quartet raises their voices with the chorus, and I square my shoulders as I assert, "I'll come clean about the entire lie first thing tomorrow. God forbid we're tied to each other any longer."

Dipping my head to cover my watery eyes, I sidestep him and set my drink next to the clutter of booze, then head toward my old room, where I left my purse. On the way, I stop Teddy, plaster on a smile, and tell him I'm leaving.

"So soon?" He furrows his brows. "We haven't even started karaoke."

"You know I'm not much of a singer." I shrug, walking backward. "Besides, Mom and Dad are too hammered already to make it to karaoke."

He chuckles, glancing at our parents, whose cheeks are flushed. "I think Dad might have fallen asleep a few times. I caught Mom snapping her fingers in front of his face."

"Keep an eye on him," I say seriously. "After the cake he had, he might go into a coma with all that sugar."

"I'll take care of him," my brother reassures me.

Before I turn away, I say, "Oh, and you'll be happy to know that I'm calling the whole online stunt with Xander quits. I'm going to post tomorrow."

"Really?" His eyebrows shoot into his hairline. "Why?"

I place both hands on my hips and try to keep my wild emotions still weighing on my chest at bay. "I thought you'd be happy, no matter the reason."

"Of course I'm… happy." He works his jaw back and forth, unconvincingly. "I just thought this was more of a long-term solution. I've kept plants alive longer than you've been 'together,' and we both know what a shitty green thumb I have."

"Turns out, this charade didn't have the effect I was hoping for," I offer and give him a one-armed hug.

As I continue down the hall, the heartache makes its way through my entire body.

I also thought Xander and I could be a long-term… *something*.

When we were together, I felt a stirring in my chest that was never there before, and I envisioned us as more than a fling. I thought we could be the real deal if we gave ourselves a chance once we returned to LA.

How very wrong I was about everything.

I've made so many mistakes the last few weeks that I have whiplash, and I'm going to spend the rest of the summer— maybe even year—trying to clean up all the chaos I've created.

While nursing a broken heart.

Because no matter how right Xander might be about me, I'm

right about him too. He's taking the easy way out by blaming me for everything, but he'll get what's coming to him.

If I'm sure of anything, it's that karma is a vengeful force of nature, and I'm counting on her to make it rain on Xander Logan.

When she's finished with Jason *Douche*, that is.

As I disappear into my old room, I finally feel like I'm out of Xander's clutches. I'm alone here without his piercing gaze following me like it's trying to tell me something that he refuses.

Either way, I have to be done with him.

The door bursts open, and Val rushes in. "What did the bastard have to say?"

"Nothing I'd like to repeat." I grab my purse and loop my arm through hers. "Did you say something about vodka at my place?"

"Ready to drown in it whenever you are." She smiles and leans into me as we make our way out to say goodbye to my parents, who slur their dismay.

And we head to my house to strategize.

Given her career as an advice columnist, Val prioritizes her brand and social media presence, and she's just the person to help me wiggle my way out of the hole I'm in.

She's also the distraction I need to keep myself from thinking about Xander and clinging to the fond memories of Maui.

Chapter 16
XANDER

My heart races more and more the longer I stare at the text.

Teddy: We need to talk

Fuck. He knows, doesn't he? He must've heard Sam and me talking at their dad's party last night, and Teddy has spent every minute since then devising a plan to completely destroy me.

I sit up in my chair, the pool in front of me dark through my sunglasses. My black sliders sting my feet when I put them on and stand, but I barely notice it.

What else could Teddy want to talk about? Did he say something at the birthday party, and I forgot? That could very well be the case since I was rather distracted, and not just by the house of comedic horrors.

Middle-aged men wearing knee-high socks.

The same crowd using the word *bosoms* more frequently than is socially acceptable.

And there was Teddy's mom's older friend from her card

group. Elaine undid a button on her shirt each time she came to ask if I wanted a drink.

I think she went home with Uncle Hubert at the end of the night.

My phone vibrates as I pace by the pool, the late-afternoon sun beating down on my bare back as if to make it clear that I can't run or hide any longer.

Teddy: Are you home

Second text without punctuation. He always uses a question mark where appropriate. He might miss a period here and there, but never a question mark.

"Christ," I mumble to the empty back yard.

My mom is still filming in Paris, and my stepdad went shopping for cars with one of his friends, who's in the market for a Camaro convertible and needed my stepdad's keen eye for expensive automobiles.

This is as good a place as any to talk to Teddy.

We have privacy, and he can kill me on the spot, if he so chooses. I wouldn't stop it.

I'd deserve it, given how I let things spiral out of control with his sister.

She looked so fucking good last night, her cheeks full of color from our trip, which was torture. It reminded me of all the times she was on top of me while we were away.

How warm and soft she felt.

Confident and untamed as she lost herself in the moment with me.

After the party last night, I convinced myself that what we had was real, especially when she said she'd come clean. I thought it was a turning point. I believed it meant I was more important to her than any damage control or public opinion.

And I really fucking need to be important to Sam.

But "first thing in the morning" as she promised has come and gone without a new announcement, so what am I supposed to think now?

Teddy: I know you're getting these, so just fucking answer me

I bite out a curse and quickly type for him to come over, then go back inside for a new drink.

Let's get this over with.

"Thanks for letting me come to the party last night. It was, um... interesting," I offer, following Teddy toward the pool chairs where I was just sitting.

He hasn't said a damn word. We walked all the way from the front door, through the foyer and expansive kitchen, and past the large portraits lining the walls and eccentric fur rugs that are always statement pieces, but Teddy stayed silent the entire damn time.

We've arrived at the pool now, and he keeps his back to me while he stares at the water.

After another long and tense pause, he whirls around and points a finger at me. "Cut the shit, okay?"

I hold my arms out and drop any charade I was stupid enough to attempt in the first place. "Let me explain."

"I don't need the details. I just need to know one thing." His intense gaze on me is unwavering, and I brace myself.

Because I'm definitely going to die today, and the last time I spoke to my mother was a week ago when I told her to behave at some fancy fashion designer's party like she's a teenager.

My final words altogether will be "Let me explain," which was a lie to begin with. How would I actually explain when I, myself, am confused about Sam?

"Do you love her?" Teddy asks.

I do a double take. "What?"

"Do you love Sam? You know—my fucking *sister*."

"What did she tell you?" I whisper.

"She didn't have to tell me anything." He frowns as he studies me like I'm some problem to solve. The pity mixed with rage in his eyes is unmistakable, and it only makes me feel worse for lying to him. "I know what happened in Maui. I know the pictures online weren't faked. You're a good writer, but there's a reason you never get in front of the camera. It's because you can't act worth a shit, and you can never hide what you're feeling. Those pictures were very real." He takes a few menacing steps toward me. "If those weren't proof enough, you've been irritatingly squirrely since you got back, and you couldn't stop mooning over her last night."

I try to catch my breath as he continues talking, his words enunciated and rushed. It's like we're in a courtroom drama, and the lawyer is giving closing statements to nail whatever son of a bitch he's after.

And he's got me up against a wall, all right.

"So, I'll ask again." He softens his stern expression a fraction, but it's not enough to ease the tension in my entire body, especially when he repeats, "Do you love her?"

I run both hands over my head and let out a rough exhale, eyeing the unfinished beer on the table next to my chair.

I need a damn drink.

"That's what I suspected," he says. "You haven't told her, have you?"

"Teddy, I want you to know that I didn't plan for anything to happen between us," I start, then sidestep him toward the pool. "Sam is just so infuriating. And strong-willed. And gorgeous. It was fucking Maui, and I wasn't thinking. I crossed a line, and I'm sorry."

"That's fine and all—and I might even believe that you're sorry—but I don't care about any of it."

"You don't?" I blink. Did I hear him correctly? There's no way he said he didn't care.

"What I care about is the fact that you hurt my sister." His lips form a grim, tight line, and my palms sweat worse than if I were literally on trial. "Let me guess—whatever was going on between you two ended when you got back because you two didn't talk about your feelings."

I give him a small nod as he comes to stand beside me, and our reflections in the water stare back at us.

We've been friends for the last three years.

He's a better friend to me than the ones I've had since high school, and Teddy's definitely the one I respect the most out of all those sons of bitches.

I've let him down in more ways than one.

I shake my head. "She doesn't know what she wants beyond a flawless online presence."

"It is her business, though. How she makes a living. I might not always understand it, but it's what she loves. She's dedicated her life to it, and I'm proud of her for putting one hundred percent into it." He smirks, his sarcasm seeping into the conversation in true Teddy fashion when he says, "In any case, it's how she's able to keep being an adult, something neither of you are acting like at the moment."

"I get that, asshole." I shove him to the side. "But it's more than that. She's afraid to let people see her imperfections, and I know that's part of social media these days. Followers want to see shiny pictures and videos of her doing cool things in and out of the gym, but..."

He glances over at me expectantly.

I sigh. "I'm not a fucking follower. I'm what's real and right in front of her, and I don't think she can be the same with me. She hasn't even told the world that she and I aren't together, like she told me she would. Sam called me a coward, but I think she had it backwards." He dips his head, and instantly, I clamp my mouth shut. "Shit, man. I know this is your sister, and I didn't mean any disrespect—"

"What're you talking about?" Teddy asks. "She's going to tell everyone you two were a lie, even though you weren't?" He searches around him, holding his head in both hands until he finds a chair behind him. Taking a seat on the edge of it, he grumbles, "Now I'm just getting fucking dizzy."

"I'm the one who's dizzy." I sit on the chair next to him and grab my drink. The bottle has dew running down the side of it, and the beer inside is warm. But I drink it, anyway. I need something—anything—to wash down the guilt knotted in my throat. "I can't believe you're not trying to drown me in this pool right now. Why are you helping me? That is what you're doing, right —helping?"

"Of course, shithead."

"Because you're such an expert in the love department?" I ask sarcastically, relieved as hell to be joking with him when I was positive this afternoon would go the opposite way.

In a much darker way than I could imagine, even as a writer of suspense and mystery thrillers.

"It's much easier to help other people than it is ourselves." He shrugs, but the gleam of amusement fades from his expression. "Love is scary as hell, man. But I think it's because we're afraid to give it to the wrong person, so we keep ourselves closed off to it until the right one comes along. Even then, it's not simple, but with the right person, it's worth it."

I hang my head, the beer sour on my tongue from the mix of emotions coursing through me.

"Why would you want her to tell everyone you're not together? Are you embarrassed of her like Jason *Douche*?" Eyes ablaze, Teddy lurches forward in his chair, and even though he's sitting, he still looks ready to rip my tiny head off, if needed.

"God, no. Please tell me you know I'm nothing like him," I plead.

His eye roll is naturally enough to convince me.

I rub a hand down the side of my face and pick my beer up again. "It's just... It's a long story, and it doesn't matter since she didn't post it this morning like she said she would."

"That's because Rico bit her."

I choke on my sip.

"Mom and Dad called her earlier to pick up their reptiles because they were too hungover to do it themselves. I had a situation of my own with a cougar's daughter who confessed she's in love with me—I'll explain later." He holds his hand up when I start to ask my many questions. "So Sam picked them up from the boarding facility, and when she tried to feed them afterward, Rico slithered his scaly ass to the top of the cage and bit her."

"Is she okay?" I jump up, my fight-or-flight kicking in like I'm the one who got bit.

"Rico isn't a venomous snake, although I wouldn't be surprised if Dad gets one of those too someday. He seems to be an equal-opportunity type of reptile owner. In any case, Sam's fine. Just scratches around her finger. We thought a piece of tooth might've actually gotten stuck in there, but the doctor ruled it out," he explains, seemingly unaffected by any of this.

"Fucking hell," I mutter, pacing next to him.

"You should talk to her," Teddy says.

"Of course." I grab my phone and scroll to our open

messages. "I need to check on her and her hand. See if she needs anything from the store. She likes those skinny margaritas..."

"Right. And after that, you should attach a note to the margaritas to tell her how much you love her."

I freeze with my thumb hovering over the *send* button. "I can't do that... I mean, I've never... What would I..." I glance up at him, my head officially a pile of mush. "That's crazy, right?"

Teddy's tone is devious with a hint of cynicism when he says, "Ah, love is crazy, haven't you heard?"

"You should tell her that you're proud of her. I think she'd appreciate it," I suggest, recalling how hurt Sam was when she talked about how her brother didn't always understand her choice to be an influencer.

"You first," he tosses back.

I scratch my chin, and before my fucking nerves get the best of me, I send the text to Sam and try not to stare at it until she responds.

Teddy said she's okay, and although I believe him, it doesn't change the fact that I'm antsy to hear from her, especially after our run-in last night.

We need to talk and figure things out.

And I need to apologize for blaming her when I'm at fault too. Because I am. How could I have been such a dick last night?

My best friend was right about love. It is scary, and opening myself up to it means I'm setting myself up for possible heartache.

But no matter what she says, I need an answer from Sam about her feelings instead of letting my imagination run rampant with all the doom it's drummed up since the festival on Maui.

It's time to put it all on the table.

I set the phone aside and turn to my friend, but I don't realize he's standing so close.

And the bastard punches me right in the gut.

"Jesus... what the fuck?" I sputter, my lungs shriveling up like a dried fruit.

"That's for sleeping with my sister in the first place. And I'll do a lot worse if you fuck this up again." He lies back on the chair and tucks his hands behind his head like he's ready to stay for a while.

I would be glad about it, but I can't decide if it's because he wants to hurt me again or not.

"I thought you were happy for us," I rasp around a cough, slinking onto the seat next to him.

"I am, but you still broke the code." He shrugs.

"Fair enough." I mimic his comfort level and lie back, my stomach already sore. "So, your girlfriend's daughter has a crush on you?"

"She told her mother she would sell her own car, cell phone, *and* scrunchie collection to be with me because she's out of her mind in love." He shakes his head. "Letting her down was not a fun conversation, but her mother still ended our fling. Apparently, I'm too much drama."

"A word that's never been used to describe you."

"That's what I said!"

"What are you going to do now?"

"Nothing. I got off easy, and it's made me think I should probably end things with Bianca too." He twists his lips like he'd rather lick the sand at Venice Beach than have that talk with her. "She's actually the one with too much drama."

"You're just not man enough to tame her." I snicker.

"Now you're just asking to be punched again."

And this is how we spend most of the day—laughing and drinking like we would during any other afternoon before Sam.

Thank fuck for that and for the fact that things aren't weird. I was so afraid they would be. Now everything's out in the open, and I still have all my fingers and toes intact, even if my stomach will be aching into next week. I definitely can't fault the guy for getting a shot in, though.

Even so, there's a Maui-sized weight that's been lifted off my damn shoulders, that's for sure.

Almost, anyway.

There's one more West I need to convince to forgive me.

Chapter 17
SAMANTHA

"Ow," I mumble as I try to raise the plate onto the bar using one hand.

My other is wrapped up from Rico's assault, and it's made me rearrange my workouts. Instead of doing shoulders and arms today like I'd originally planned, I'm sneaking a leg workout into my schedule.

Which turns out perfectly since leg days are the best days. It's why I sell tanks and cropped shirts with that phrase plastered across the chest. I'm not alone in my thinking, either, since it's my third bestselling item.

I have yet to figure out what to do about my top selling one.

The #GymBae merch is still selling like crazy, and my website has even crashed a few times from the overload of visitors in the last week.

I should be stoked. Over the moon. Throwing myself a party every night with those numbers.

But all I did last night was drink, and this morning, I nursed my wounded hand like I did my ego.

With all of Rico's excitement, I didn't have the time or energy to make the video I promised Xander I would. Jason and his followers are still tagging me for a response to his video, provoking me into playing their stupid games.

All so that Jason can gain a few new fans at my expense.

Just like Xander.

The video outing our little ploy is sure to get him major sympathy points. They'll leave my page and flock to his like magnets.

So many people are against me right now for what started out as an honest mistake. There are so many more who have forgiven me and forgotten all about it, and although I'm trying to focus on them since they're the ones who matter, I'm losing my fucking patience—and mind.

"You could tell the truth. The whole story," Val suggested last night after the party, and now her words run through my mind like they're on a loop or in an Instagram boomerang.

Over and over.

The freaking truth.

I want to do that, but how? What would I actually say? And what then—everyone moves on?

People obviously don't let things go very easily.

A month ago, I was happy and successful, and now all I do is try to pick up the pieces of a broken business.

The worst part about it all is... Xander.

I let him and myself down, and I lost him.

That's where the truth lies, doesn't it? With Xander Logan.

And if I share every last detail of us, it'll just mean it's really over. That the ending of our trip was the end of what we had.

That's the realization I had last night while I talked to Val. I'm reluctant to give us up, no matter what arguments we've had. No matter what mistakes we've made.

I'm not afraid of my followers moving on and forgetting the whole thing—I'm concerned about doing this myself because I refuse to believe Xander isn't the one for me.

The honest truth is that I miss him.

I miss laughing with him. Making silly bets and teasing each other.

I miss being in his arms.

"Focus," I mutter to myself and duck under the bar until it rests across my shoulders. I push onto my toes to unrack the weight and walk it backward, each step steady and strong.

Inhaling, I sink into a squat, my quads screaming as I reach the bottom of my position, and I rise again on an exhale. The only thing I think about while I complete my set is my body and my breathing.

The rest of the gym and world continue around me while I lose myself in the movement—my happy place.

Sweat trickles down my neck and stomach, and my calves tremble as I walk the bar back to the rack, careful not to use my hurt hand to lift it off my shoulders.

And the nagging thoughts come barreling back into my mind as if to ask, "Did you think it'd be that easy to forget us?"

I blow out a frustrated breath, and when I spin around, I come face-to-face with Jason and his smug grin.

"Surprised to see you here," he says, nudging my shoulder with his as he steps around me toward the rack. He slings his bag onto the floor next to mine, then faces me again, his eyebrows raised.

"I'm a member here. It's just as much my gym as anyone else's." I wave around the room, the sun from the open garage door shining on me like a spotlight.

And the hair on the back of my neck rises.

"I just didn't think you'd ever come out of hiding with all the embarrassing shit going around." He crosses his arms over his chest and gives me a once-over. "Where is your *boyfriend*, anyway?"

The mocking way he says the word grates on every last

nerve. The ass is enjoying his attempt at making me squirm, but I refuse to let him have that kind of control over me anymore.

The last straw snaps when he laughs and removes a plate from the end of the bar, making my eye twitch.

"I'm not finished here," I say in a low but firm tone.

"I think you're done," he asserts over his shoulder, then puts the plate down and spins toward me again. "You're done here and online. No one in the fitness industry respects you anymore."

I pinch the bridge of my nose and laugh. "You're trying awfully hard to make me look like some loser who should just give up," I throw back, stepping up to him and meeting him chest to chest. "Seems to me like you're the loser who's heavily intimidated by a strong woman. Especially one who's stronger than you in every fucking sense of the word."

He scoffs. "That's a stretch."

"You think so? Then answer me this—why were you so adamant about keeping us a secret when I didn't want to? Why did you insist on showing off your female friends but never once posted a picture of you next to me? Obviously, you want attention, given how hard you've milked my mistakes the last few weeks. What could be the reasoning?"

I tap my chin with exaggeration, then cut him off before he has a chance to respond, taking another step toward him and forcing him backward with every word. "Here's what I think— you wanted me to fail to make yourself feel better. You were waiting desperately for it. All because you're an insecure man who's as small and puny as his dick."

There's a low hum from behind me, which is when I realize we've attracted an audience.

An audience with camera phones pointed right to us.

Shit.

Jason stumbles over the plate he removed from the bar, and

the arrogant confidence he walked up to me with is nowhere to be found.

Even when he rights himself, he stands just a little shorter than before.

"Now here's what's going to happen." I wave over the plate and nod toward the bar. "You're going to put that back where I had it, and then you're going to leave me the hell alone. Don't tag me on social media. Don't utter my name to your followers or friends. Forget you and I ever breathed the same air at all. I already have."

Jason peers over my shoulder at the crowd still huddled around us, but I don't turn. I stare him down as my blood continues boiling, and my chest heaves, courtesy of the adrenaline coursing through me from finally telling him off.

"Listen, baby, can we talk about this somewhere else?" he whispers to me, his eyes still stuck on the people.

"*Now,*" I grind out and stand my ground.

Frowning, he crouches down, picks up the plate, and racks it. Then he grabs his bag and storms out of here with a sad entourage of only a couple people behind him.

He completes the whole sequence faster than he gulps down his pre-workout, and the sudden sensation that floods my body is pretty damn exhilarating.

The mixture of relief and hope and pride and everything in between is overwhelming, and I feel like I just ran two marathons back-to-back.

The second I turn around, many people hold their fists up for me to bump and congratulate me on standing up for myself. Some women even call me a "queen" and ask to hug me.

While I wouldn't call myself the latter, I'm caught up in the celebration and happy to have finally put Jason is his fucking place.

I didn't run, hide, or shrink back in order to make him feel better.

I stood tall, and that's worth celebrating.

But the laughter and cheers cease to exist for me when my eyes land on Xander. Where did he come from?

As the crowd disperses, he's the only one left in place, working his jaw back and forth while he watches me.

"What're you doing here?" I ask cautiously. "I figured you would've burst into flames the moment you walked through the door, so you obviously risked your well-being for something important."

His lip slightly twitches. "I'm not allergic to the gym. In fact, I spend five nights a week at my gym. I just don't work out while I'm on vacation."

I gulp to wet my dry throat at the thought of Maui. The *vacation* that changed my life.

The word will never be the same for me.

"What do you want?" I ask weakly.

He waves his arms around the scene of excitement. "That was..."

I place my trembling hands on my hips, my heart still pounding from the commotion.

"Incredible," he finishes on an exhale.

His praise catches me off guard, and suddenly, I'm tongue-tied.

"Did you get my text?" Xander drops his gaze down to my hand. "Teddy told me what happened with Rattle—I mean, Rico. Fuck, I can't keep them straight." He scratches the back of his head, his T-shirt rising above the waistband of his pants with the movement. "I thought I was the one with bad luck around animals."

I fight a smile and start to settle into the ease of how we used to be, but I catch myself. "Wait, what did you say to Teddy?"

"Everything." As the breath is knocked out of me, he crosses the space between us and grips my arms. "Sam, I'm sorry for what I said last night and for how I acted the last night of our trip. It takes so much courage to put yourself out there for literally millions, and you were so amazing just now with Jason. I seriously almost jumped in to punch him in the jaw for being such an asshole, but you took him down without laying a finger on him." He chuckles and cups my cheek, his touch familiar and comforting. "You show up for your followers, but you do a damn good job of showing up for yourself too."

I lean into his palm, and my angry resolve crumbles like a trail of dominoes. "Xander, I'm—hang on, what did you just say?" Blinking rapidly, I try to bring him back into focus as my heart rate picks up again.

But for a different reason.

"That you show up for yourself? I really admire that—"

"Oh my God, that's it. That's what I should do." I grip his forearms and look into his confused eyes.

But I've never seen more clearly, nor have I ever felt so sure about something than I do about the idea he just gave me.

It's the answer I've been looking for to what's holding me back with my career.

"You're a genius," I say to Xander and jump back, scoop my bag up from the dusty floor with streaks of white chalk across the mat, and squeal. "Thank you!"

"For what?" he asks.

"I have to take care of something right now." I kiss his cheek, pausing briefly when my lips touch his warm skin, electricity passing between us. "I'll call you later, and we'll talk. Promise."

He nods, and I race out of the gym faster than any sprinting session I've completed. Each step I take grows bouncier as I reach my car and throw the door open. Sliding inside, I'm still wearing my smile like an accessory, and I never want it to dull again.

Especially not because I gave so much control to an asshole like Jason.

This is my life, and I'm taking charge of it again.

Chapter 18
XANDER

She blew me off... I think.

Sam didn't answer my text about her hand, and I thought I might've been too late.

So, I went after the girl. Isn't that what I was supposed to do? How every romantic comedy goes? Except I didn't have the chance to confess my love for her because she blew me off.

That's not a good sign for any happy ending.

But Sam also kissed me on the cheek and said she'd call me.

Which she hasn't, and it's been a whole day.

I've jogged a couple miles, had dinner with Klein at a pretentious restaurant with food portions the size of my big toe, and slept a full two hours since I last saw her.

And not a fucking word from Sam since.

What the hell am I supposed to think about that?

Pacing a hole in the carpet, I clutch my phone in a crushing grip, murmuring to myself.

Fuck, I'm pining.

This is what pining looks like. It's exactly what I used to tease Easton Garrett over in college. He was in love with a girl, and he moped for weeks after she dumped him, eating nothing but ramen noodles and cold pizza.

I never understood him until now—the poor bastard.

Then again, he's not so pitiful now. Just the opposite. Easton's a bigshot and spends every night at some premier club, partying with New York's finest. From what I can tell online and the pictures of him standing next to Carter Fields, the billionaire CEO of Fields Company, I'd say he got over his college girlfriend and probably doesn't even remember her name.

Sam isn't easily forgettable. She's funny and full of life.

Sexy as hell, especially when she's telling off scumbags.

I rub my twitching lips as I continue pacing the living room, recalling the way Sam shot Jason down yesterday like he was one of those targets at the ax throwing places.

And she launched her weapons right smack into the bullseye.

The way he raced out of the gym, his tail practically tucked between his legs, was so comical that I called Teddy the moment I left to tell him all about it.

He'd already seen the whole thing online, though. Coincidentally, he was just about to call me, but I beat him to it.

In any case, he and I have jokes for years to come, thanks to Jason *Douche*.

Sighing, I stick my phone in my back pocket and head out to the patio, where I left my laptop and character notebook. Between the pages, I've jotted down a web of ideas and notes from Maui, and if I were to rip them all out and post them to my wall, I'd look like a serial killer for sure.

Outside, I sit at the table and get back to work on the script I've been piecing together, but I spend most of the morning just trying to decipher my scribbles.

As if my handwriting wasn't bad enough, some of the ink is smudged from saltwater and Bloody Marys.

So, I fill in the blanks from memory as best I can for this new project I started as soon as I returned—a satirical romantic comedy about a guy and a girl who run away from their problems to an island, where they encounter quirky but conspiratorial couples and sea turtles. The couple falls in love during the little moments in between this grand adventure.

I'm writing about Sam and myself.

It's a mix of us both—romantic and funny with a dash of my brand of suspense, tied into pages of a unique parody.

All the elements fit like Sam and I do.

I'm in so much damn trouble over this girl.

For hours, I cross out notes I can't use and replace them with other ideas, my attention alternating between the script and my phone.

Still no damn word from Sam.

No new posts to her social media or stories.

No text or call or fucking clue that she still knows I exist.

And I've been stuck on the same scene for the last half hour because I can't stop checking my phone long enough to write anything worth a shit.

I would take crappy words if it meant I wrote *something*, but no such luck.

The sun has already set by the time my phone vibrates with a text from Teddy. Assuming it's another meme to describe Jason's assholery, I ignore it.

But then I get another.

And another.

The last is a text using all caps, so I finally close my laptop, and with a shaking thumb, I click the link he sent me.

Sam's face fills the screen, and my chest swells. She's glowing. Her smile is wide and uncontainable as she talks into the camera, her hair thrown over one shoulder and face free of makeup except for a touch of mascara.

Her voice is clear and comfortable, and her confidence radiates through the phone. She's always commanded the camera, but it's different in this video.

She seems more relaxed, and it puts me at ease too.

"The last few weeks have been pretty crazy, right?" she says into the camera, which moves as she goes through her kitchen. "You don't even know the half of it, but I'm posting here to tell you every last juicy detail."

I rest my elbows on the table, following her through the kitchen in the background like I'm tracing the pattern of an earthquake on a map.

Where is she going with this?

"Hey, kiddo," Klein calls out, and the sound of a door sliding closed follows him. "Up for a game of Scrabble?"

"Not right now," I answer absentmindedly, my focus glued to the things Sam is saying in the video.

She's talking about everything—Jason, Maui, *me*.

And fuck, do her eyes light up when she mentions my name, even though she's telling everyone the truth about how our relationship started and that she's sorry she misled them.

"I started this account with no more than fifty followers a few years ago," she continues. "But somewhere along the way to a couple million, I lost sight of why I began this journey in the first place, and I don't want to keep going down that path. I want to stay true to who I am and what I want for my mind and body, and I want to encourage you all to do the same."

I smile as Klein slips back inside somewhere behind me without another word.

"Someone I care deeply about reminded me yesterday that we need to show up for ourselves, whether that means our fitness and well-being, jobs, friends, whatever—*show up*." She inhales like she's preparing herself for something, and it's obvious there's an announcement coming.

I lean close to the phone like I can travel through it and be there with her, because the fact that I know she's talking about me being the someone she cares deeply about makes me so fucking relieved.

I'm proud when she says, "So, I'll be launching a new campaign with all-new merch in my store. I'm calling it Be Your Own Gym Bae, and I have a sneak peek of the logo on my website. I'll also have new workout plans that are catered to different lifestyles—new home routines, quick and effective circuits for the gym, and more. Click the link in my bio to check it out, and stay tuned for all the details. Until then, stay happy and healthy. Talk soon, fam."

She signs off, and I'm left stunned.

It's perfect.

She's not giving up just because she had a setback—she's standing up stronger, instead.

And fuck if that doesn't make Sam even sexier.

I grab my stuff off the table and head back inside, where I set it on the counter. I've just grabbed my keys by the door when the doorbell echoes across the high ceilings. The sound of that damn bell feels like it comes from inside my head, loud and intimidating.

I swing it open and freeze. "Sam."

"Hi." She fidgets with her fingers in front of her.

The red tank top she wears is simple—it would be on anyone else, anyway—but on her, the color pops against her summer complexion, bringing out the blush in her cheeks too.

As she shifts her weight, she seems nervous, and I'm not sure if that's a good thing or not.

"Come in?" I say, but it comes out as more of a question.

Nodding, she brushes past me and into the ridiculously

extravagant foyer. Seriously, the area is larger than the dining room, and no one even uses this space.

My mother barely uses the entire house, actually.

"Are you home alone?" Sam asks, spinning in place to face me.

"I, um..." I blink. *What did she say?*

"Is your mom back from Paris yet?"

"Oh, she'll be back next week. Klein is around here somewhere, I think." I run a hand over my head, extra aware of how strong my feelings for Sam are now that she's standing right in front of me.

The sudden nerves are tying my fucking tongue up like a knotted rope.

"Klein is just leaving," my stepdad announces, poking his head around the corner from the hall. "I'll see you two later."

With a wink, he disappears again, and a few seconds later, the clicking of the side door drifts over us.

"The answer to your question, then, is that yes, we are alone," I joke, and it earns me a glorious giggle, soft and free of the tension we've had this week.

"When will you move back into your place?"

"Teddy found my friend Calder a place, which he'll be able to move into at the end of this month, so I'll get it back then. Fingers crossed I can stay sane until then."

She waves her arms around. "How can you ever tell if anyone else is here in the first place?"

"Oh, I can tell." I roll my eyes.

What is she thinking?

"Do you want a drink or anything?" I offer as she bites her bottom lip, drawing my attention to the exact spot her teeth sink into her plump lip, and I fight a groan.

This is a new form of torture I never knew could make me

suffer this badly. My body is more fucking tense than a pulled muscle.

"Sure, but I want to talk to you first, if that's okay."

Nodding, I lead her toward the kitchen, and the air shifts. We've gone from being friends to sleeping together to fighting like two birds in a cage, but now we're... I don't know.

In limbo? That seems like the only way to put it.

In the kitchen, I reach into the refrigerator and grab a beer for her, but before I can hand it over, she whirls around, wringing the front of her shirt with her fingers. "You were totally right about me, and I didn't want to hear it. I was too blinded by things that shouldn't have mattered to admit it to you or myself, and I'm sorry."

I shut the door to the fridge and lean against it. "I saw the video."

"You did?" she asks, surprise written all over her.

"I'm happy for you," I whisper, my lips twitching when she gulps.

She has no idea how proud of her I am, does she? Which makes me wonder about the guys she's dated in the past, although Jason should've been a perfect indication to begin with.

In any case, Sam obviously has never been with a guy who truly values her, and I want to change that.

I'll do anything to change that.

"Thank you," she says, locking eyes with me.

The ice maker kicks on in the freezer behind me, and the cubes drop like a glass shattering, making us both jump.

As we share a laugh, she accepts the beer from me and furrows her brows. "I'm also sorry I never called you yesterday. Why were you at the gym, anyway?"

My grin fades as I sober up—I guess we're doing this.

No going back, not that I want to.

"I needed to…" I blow out a breath and scratch the back of my head. "I needed to tell you that I'm a coward."

"That's basically what I'm admitting. Kinda stepping on my toes here," she says on a laugh and sways ever so slightly, reminding me of the way the breeze swept over her dresses while we were on Maui. "I guess we were both scared of getting hurt again," she whispers.

"I was afraid I'd be a much better fake boyfriend than a real one, and I never told you how I felt." I swallow around the lump in my throat as the cabinets, lights, and the rest of the kitchen fade.

I didn't think this would be so difficult, but when she smiles and takes a step toward me, I realize it doesn't need to be so hard, after all.

Not with Sam.

"What are you saying now? That you want to be my real boyfriend?" she asks, tilting her head to the side in a coy way that causes a strain in my pants.

I slip my hand into hers, palm against palm, and I hold on tight as I take a leap. "If you'll have me."

The words are barely out of my mouth before she launches herself into my embrace, wrapping her arms around my neck and fusing her lips to mine in a kiss that's almost painful.

But very right.

It's always felt right with Sam.

I was an idiot to think she was anything like the women I've met in the past. Sam is nothing like them at all, and I'm not going to let fear stand in my way again when it comes to her.

I grab a fistful of Sam's hair and tug her closer.

More.

"You always taste so fucking sweet, Sam," I growl into her mouth.

And I can feel her aroused moan down to my dick so strongly that I jerk backward, bringing her with me.

We stumble from wall to wall, rattling drawers in the kitchen and the paintings hanging on the walls in the hallway, our tongues tangled together the entire time.

We're frantic and eager to reacquaint ourselves.

"Come here." I pull us into the nearest open room, and as we resume our kiss in the dark, I feel around behind me until my hand lands on something solid.

My body buzzes as I hoist her onto the edge of a hard surface, then blink around—we're in the dining room.

Sam's sitting on the table with her legs spread for me like a meal—one I'm ready to devour.

"Xander," she whispers as she jerks me toward her by my shirt, the thin material about to tear in her firm grasp like my resolve. I wouldn't stop it, either, but she sounds like she has something more to say.

"What is it, gorgeous?" I place a kiss on her shoulder and start to make my way up the column of her neck, but she cups my cheek and pulls my face up to hers.

"I love you," she confesses, and the wind is knocked out of me.

In the best fucking way possible.

"I don't know if that's crazy, or—" she rambles, but I cut her off with a scorching hot kiss that I hope she feels in her damn soul.

Because I feel it in mine.

"I love you too, Sam," I say against her swollen lips. "Sam West or Samantha Ray—I love all of you."

She smiles against me, her mouth pressed along the scruff of my jaw as she fumbles with the button on my pants.

Her fingers are cold against my hot skin, but it doesn't bother me—I just need her.

The woman I love.

The one who feels the same.

I've never been with someone I truly love like this, and the moment we're free of the barriers between us, my pants wrapped around my ankles, I sink into her, reveling in this feeling of ecstasy.

I roll my hips and savor this moment, knowing it's already ingrained in my memory forever.

Leaning my forehead to hers, I inhale the sweet smell of coconut and sex as I pull out and thrust back into her tight, wet heat, her thighs trembling around my waist.

"Yes, Xander," she breathes, her pants echoing in my ear. "More. Give me more."

"Always." I kiss her again as I pull out, the cold air skimming over my soaked dick and causing a jolt to my nervous system. Heart pumping, I stand upright, throw her legs onto both my shoulders, and slide back inside her.

The soft and smooth skin of her legs rubs against my jaw as I rock my hips into her, loving how sexy this position is.

She squeezes my rigid length more tightly, and the friction makes me see stars as the anticipation builds.

My abs clench more and more painfully with each thrust.

The sounds of our slick skin slapping as we come together echoes in the silent room, and although we're alone in this house, we might as well be the only ones in the world.

Whether we're on Maui, in LA, or out in fucking space, Sam and I will always be one.

Because her face in the dim moonlight streaming in from between the curtains of the far window is all I see.

She's all I feel.

Sam is the only one my heart beats this quickly for.

With my name on her sultry lips, she cries out as her body

writhes against the hard wooden surface of the table, her arms spread out to her sides to grip the edges.

"Fuck," I hiss and fall forward with my own climax, my balls squeezing tight as I come with the force of the last seven nights that I spent without her.

My vision is blurred, and I hang on to her strong legs still wrapped around my head to steady myself.

"Wow," she says, her voice raspy like she spent all night screaming—and I plan to make her scream some more, all right.

"Jesus," I whisper, licking my lips and matching her response. "Come here."

I gently unhook her ankles from behind my neck and help her stand upright. Once she's balanced, I run my knuckles up to her cheek and place a soft, lingering kiss to her mouth.

"That was... just wow." She pants and brings her hands to rest on my chest, peering up at me through dazed and sparkling eyes.

"Agreed." I chuckle, smoothing her hair back. "Let's get you changed. I have plans for us."

"Plans?" she asks. It's an idle question, although there's plenty of confusion too.

"Sex in the shower. Duh." I interlock my fingers through hers and lead her away, but I catch sight of her shorts and panties thrown to the corner and abruptly stop. "Actually, we should probably clean up in here before Klein comes back. This is where we eat, after all."

"I'll give you something to eat..."

"You are going to be the death of me." I shake my head, then kiss her.

Hopping toward the light switch, I pull my feet the rest of the way out of my pants, which I then use to wipe any remnants of the mess we just made, and she bursts into laughter behind me.

"You can't seriously call that cleaning!"

I shrug. "Good enough for now."

She rolls her eyes and skips out of the room, then comes back with a spray cleaner and paper towels.

"Aren't you proper," I deadpan.

Over her shoulder, she tsks at me. "Do I look proper to you?" She bends at the waist and gives me a mischievous grin, which is when I realize she's still not wearing any pants.

And her ass is on full display.

She did this on purpose, and holy fuck, cleaning has never been hotter.

"I'm done." She straightens back up and sways toward me.

"But I'm not done with you," I say, my voice rugged.

"Good." She quirks a brow and brushes past me.

I chase her up the stairs to my room, and we fall onto my bed together, a mess of laughter and hormones.

The glow of the setting sun through my window sends a warm current through my body. Another day has come and gone, but I won't be spending any more without Sam by my side. No more nights in an empty bed or hollow void.

She's filled it completely—and then some.

As I hum happily under my breath, she flips onto her side and runs her finger up my arm. "Does this mean we're official?"

I snicker. "We can change our relationship statuses online after a shower."

"Deal." She grins and races into the bathroom.

Rubbing a hand down my face and over my curling lips, I follow her, enjoying the bounce in her bare ass as she wiggles out of the rest of her clothes.

And all I can think is that going to Maui was definitely the best damn idea I've ever had.

Epilogue

SAMANTHA

Next summer...

I step out onto our balcony, and the refreshing breeze skates across my cheek, immediately soothing me.

I don't have anything to be stressed about at the moment, but this view and perfect weather are doing wonders for my soul, nonetheless.

It's been a wild year, and this is our reward—a relaxing vacation on Maui for the second year in a row.

The calm before the next storm.

Xander and I are thinking about making it an annual tradition, but it depends on what the upcoming year will bring in terms of schedules.

I launched my Be Your Own Gym Bae athletic wear, and it's been such a huge success that I've started my own clothing company. One that stands tall for strong women—and sells squat-proof leggings. We also have our own headquarters that isn't in my living room, and it's growing into something I only ever dreamed of.

The number of influencers who applied to be a rep for the Ray of Sunshine line shook me from the inside out. I was blown away by the responses and by the love of what we stand for.

And although the final decision for reps was difficult, I'm proud of the team we've cultivated. They're from all over the country, and I hope to expand into overseas territories soon too.

But that's in the future.

Right now, I'm focusing on maintaining the momentum of our launch.

We had our version of a grand opening last month with the whole team. Our friends and family also attended, and it was an event to remember.

Amazing drinks and food with the best people I've grown close enough with to call family.

Music and dancing.

Xander by my side.

He looked so good in his tux that I'm surprised I kept my hands off him until we got home that night.

We barely made it through the door before we clawed at each other. I don't think we even fully undressed out of our fancy attire before Xander pressed my back against the door and had his way with me.

We've been hot and heavy like that since last summer, but we've turned up the sex-ometer since we moved in together six months ago. Although Teddy wasn't super thrilled to find out we're *that* serious, as he put it, sharing an address with Xander has helped our relationship. We both work long hours, and it's nice, to say the least, to fall into our bed at the end of the day together.

Otherwise, we'd spend our free time driving across LA to see each other—no, thank you.

Xander's muffled voice drifts out to the balcony as he continues talking on the phone with a producer about the screenplay he optioned.

My boyfriend, the screenwriter.

He fucking did it, as I always knew he would.

And the fact that he sold the screenplay based on our previous trip to Maui—the one where we fell in love—makes the whole thing that much sweeter.

"All right," he says into the phone, his voice louder, like he's walking toward me. "Yes. Okay. Talk soon."

I feel him before he reaches me and runs his finger down my arm, heat radiating off him in waves. "Hi, gorgeous," he whispers in my ear, then places a kiss to my temple.

I sigh with so much contentment that I might as well be high, leaning into him as warmth envelopes me from his embrace.

"You look absolutely stunning in this dress," he murmurs with a squeeze of his arms around my waist.

"You said the same thing about my dolphin pajamas yesterday."

"And I meant it, too." His low chuckle vibrates down my body, tickling me.

Awareness tingles down my spine, and all I want is for him to strip this dress right off me.

I lift my arm and cup his cheek in my palm behind me, then tangle my fingers through his wavy hair.

Following my lead, Xander uses his thumb and forefinger to angle my chin upward, and he covers my mouth with his, immediately parting my lips with his tongue as if he can't get enough of me.

Some days, it feels like he can't, and I love that about him —about us.

He's the first man to ever make me feel worthy and sexy, whether I'm in sweats or a sparkling gown.

He's a big reason I'm confident in myself like never before.

I no longer put so much pressure on myself to look perfect online. In fact, it's been part of my new brand to own my flaws and imperfections.

Because they're actually my strengths.

I now post videos and pictures of me during all parts of my workouts, even when I'm soaked in sweat from head to toe and limping between machines during a brutal leg session.

I've learned to accept it all and find beauty in my crazy hair and sweaty outlines on my pants and bras. Because I'm strong and capable, and I challenge myself to live my best life.

To live healthy and happy from the inside out.

And it fills my heart with joy that Xander not only respects and supports it, but he also cheers me on and loves me even more for it.

"Walk with me," he whispers.

"Where—inside and straight to the bed?" I ask, smiling around my cheeky response.

"There will definitely be time for that, but I want to show you something in the garden first."

He grips my hand and leads me back inside, closing the door behind us on the way.

"I'm still paranoid about wild hogs racing into our rooms, even though we're on the fourth floor this time." He lets out a soft laugh, and we continue on our way, hand in hand.

Out in the garden behind the hotel, pink, yellow, and white hibiscus flowers poke out of the lush greenery like nosy neighbors, but a lot friendlier and more welcoming.

I planted a few of my own, along with a couple of bird of paradise flowers, in the garden at our place. They're the first things I see when I leave the house, and it always reminds me of our first summer on Maui together.

They're symbols of the future Xander and I are building together. After all, hibiscus represents unity and peace, and the bird of paradise is for love and thoughtfulness.

It's the good energy we like to surround ourselves with, and they make the place feel more like *our* home.

It's quiet in the garden here, except for a soft melody coming through the hotel's speakers.

Xander and I are the only ones around, walking along the path in the middle of the garden, a big stone fountain at the end with water falling from the top.

"Let's sit for a minute," he instructs, and we sit thigh to thigh on the edge of the fountain, which is thicker than I expected.

I scoot my dress down and cross my leg over the other as I swipe my hair out of my face to get a better look at him.

His smile is hesitant and shy, and no matter how long I've known Xander, this obvious vulnerability will always make my heart flutter.

It usually means he's going to say or do something that will make me love him more.

He retrieves a piece of paper from inside his jacket pocket and hands the crinkly sheet to me, his fingers noticeably shaking. "The list," he rasps.

"Oh my God." I unfold the sheet of paper that I haven't seen since last summer like I'm unraveling an ancient and valuable map.

"I thought we could finish it this time around."

My eyes blur as I run my finger over our handwriting.

We were just a couple of lost souls then. Two people who found their way in the world when they found each other.

"But we already completed—" My voice catches in my throat as I turn the paper over and find the words "Will you marry me?" scrolled across the back in his barely legible handwriting.

My laugh is shaky as I lift my gaze and find Xander down on one knee, the setting sun casting a pinkish glow over him.

And the ring he holds between his thumb and forefinger sparkles between us.

"I love you, Sam," he says, his voice thick with emotion. "This last year with you has been the best of my life, and I want more. I want to be side by side as we continue kicking ass and taking over LA."

I giggle and swipe a joyful tear from the corner of my eye.

"I want more adventures with you. More laughs and arguments over healthy foods. I want to live this wild life with you. Will you marry me?" His sharp inhale is deafening and so sweet. "Xander." I sniffle and clutch my chest. "You've made me feel like myself again—a better version of it, actually. You've made me so happy, and I'd love nothing more than to be your wife."

He stands and tilts my head back to kiss me.

When he slides the ring onto my finger, he smirks. "Nothing more official than this, right?"

"Exactly." My laugh is carefree and loud as I hold my hand up, and we both admire my ring.

The backdrop of the garden and the island beyond is lively and beautiful, and this is officially my favorite moment with him.

THE END

Want more of Samantha and Xander? Grab your **FREE bonus epilogue** at https://bit.ly/3NA5ltG

Also by Georgia Coffman

Stuck with You Series

Stuck with the Billionaire

Stuck at Christmas

Stuck with the Movie Star

Stuck with the Boss

Stuck Under the Mistletoe

Stuck with You Spinoff Series

Stuck with a Date

Stuck with the Rock Star

The Heat Series

Falling for a Stranger

Falling for a Player

Falling for a Bachelor

Falling for My Roommate

A Standalone Novel

Official

KB Worlds

Heartbeat

The Salvation Society

Unbreakable

Acknowledgments

As always, a huge shoutout to YOU, sweet reader, for picking up this book. Whether this is the first or tenth story you've read from me, I appreciate you taking a chance on this romcom. By doing so, you've made my dreams come true!

I'd like to thank the beach in Gulf Shores, Alabama. I spent hours sitting in a chair with my toes buried in the sand and my laptop perched on my lap as I wrote the first half of this book. It was scenic, peaceful, and inspiring. Every wave and call of a seagull pulled the words out of me with ease. This place motivated me to write Xander and Sam's love story, and it'll always be special.

On that note, thank you to the two ladies I've called friends for almost ten years now, Shelby and Mary Beth. You took me on the beach trip, and you two have supported me and this writing thing from the very beginning. A million times, thank you.

Thanks to my KKSB girls as well—Chelle, Julia, Mae, and Claire. I can't write books without y'all, and I'm so glad I don't have to. Chelle, you gave me the idea to give Samantha a book to begin with, and from there, this book sprouted wings. Julia, you answered all my questions about Maui, and I truly appreciate your help.

To my mom, I can't say thank you enough. You always believe in me, no matter what, and you've taught me to believe in myself. I'll forever be grateful for your love and support.

To my husband—my forever partner, cheerleader, and go-to guy for all the laughs. You gave me the courage to do this thing, and it means so much to me that you are excited for every step of this journey. Life with you is my favorite adventure. Love you, forever and always.

About the Author

Georgia Coffman is an author of steamy contemporary romance. She has a Master's in Professional Writing and loves the TV show *Friends*, as well as shopping. She and her husband enjoy working out and playing with their two pups. Georgia loves to connect on social media or through email, so feel free to reach out with any questions, your fave book recommendations, or even a funny joke!

Newsletter – www.georgiacoffman.com/newsletter
Facebook – https://geni.us/GeorgiaFB
Instagram – https://geni.us/GeorgiaIG
TikTok https://geni.us/GeorgiaTT

Pinterest – https://geni.us/GeorgiaPinterest
Goodreads – https://geni.us/GeorgiaGR
BookBub – https://geni.us/GeorgiaBB
Amazon - https://geni.us/GeorgiaAmazon
Verve Romance - https://geni.us/GeorgiaVerve